CAT
IN THE
CITY

CAT IN THE CITY

JULIE SALAMON

Illustrations by Jill Weber

DIAL BOOKS FOR YOUNG READERS

An imprint of Penguin Group (USA) LLC

DIAL BOOKS FOR YOUNG READERS
Published by the Penguin Group
Penguin Group (USA) LLC
375 Hudson Street
New York, New York 10014

USA / Canada / UK / Ireland / Australia / New Zealand / India / South Africa / China
penguin.com
A Penguin Random House Company

Text copyright © 2014 by Julie Salamon
Pictures copyright © 2014 by Jill Weber

Library of Congress Cataloging-in-Publication Data

Salamon, Julie.
Cat in the city / by Julie Salamon ; illustrations by Jill Weber.
pages   cm
Summary: As he tries to make his own way in New York City, a handsome stray cat that becomes known as Pretty Boy finds a series of temporary homes while learning that relying on others, and being relied upon, is a wonderful thing.
ISBN 978-0-8037-4056-3 (hardcover)
[1. Cats—Fiction. 2. Human-animal relationships—Fiction. 3. Dogs—Fiction. 4. New York (N.Y.)—Fiction.] I. Weber, Jill, illustrator. II. Title.
PZ7.S1474Cat 2014
[Fic—dc23
2013013439

Manufactured in China on acid-free paper

1 3 5 7 9 10 8 6 4 2

Designed by Jill Weber
Text set in Charlotte Std

CAT IN THE CITY
IS DEDICATED TO:

HARRY HOUDINI   SADIE   MAGGIE   KURO

CONTENTS

CAT
IN THE
CITY

Through these arches

our eyes
our hearts
dwell
in the days
of wonder

—Hannah Gray

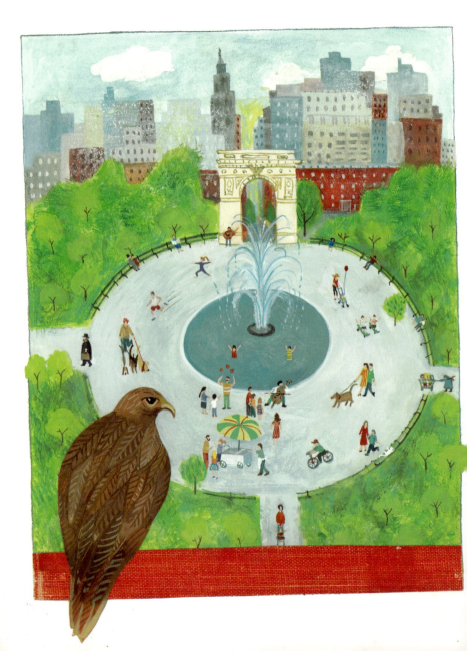

CHAPTER ONE

Morning in Washington Square

A large, powerful bird gazed downward with the fierce eyes of a hunter. He was a red-tailed hawk and his stomach was empty. Peering at the rectangular field far below, he saw many small animals that would make a tasty breakfast. But he didn't move a feather. Timing was everything and the right moment hadn't arrived.

From his perch on the roof of the Bobst Library, overlooking Washington Square, the hawk had a clear view of the Empire State Building. He cocked his head slightly, listening to the sounds of the city waking up.

His eyes scanned the park's graceful walkways. He checked out lampposts and trees from top to bottom. All he needed was one careless squirrel, or an absent-minded pigeon. The hawk was so hungry he would even settle for a large rat.

Children's voices floated skyward from a playground. The hawk ignored them. He also wasn't interested in the musicians playing their instruments by the grand fountain, or the old woman pushing a cart piled high with empty cans and bottles, or the students practicing yoga in front of the Washington Square Arch. Likewise, he didn't turn toward the yaps and barks coming from the dog run, where pets could play without being leashed to their owners. They were all too big for him to wrap his claws around.

The hawk grew impatient. His eyes darted back and forth, forth and back. His gaze flitted past something that looked like a wrung-out mop. Then he decided to take a closer look. The mop was a large cat sprawled out on a bench.

Finally! thought the hawk.

Every instinct told him that this fellow was an easy mark. His fur once was white, but now it was gray, dirty, and tangled. His eyes were shut tight.

What a lazy bum, was the hawk's fleeting thought as he shook his head in disapproval.

His harsh judgment was unfair. The cat was simply worn-out. He had arrived in Washington Square in the middle of the night and hadn't slept a wink. He was new to this part of the city and had never spent the night in the park before. Even for a streetwise fellow like him, it was terrifying. Every sound was magnified in the dark. Every rustling became ominous. Who knew what enemies could pounce out of the shadows? After pacing around the fountain and creeping along dimly lit paths all night long, he was a nervous wreck—and exhausted.

Now that the sun was up, this very tired cat planned to lie on the bench all day, enjoying the warmth. Just the thought made him happy.

He had one agenda; the hawk had another.

Sleep, thought the cat as he drifted off.

Delicious! thought the red-tailed hawk as he prepared to make his move.

Seconds later, the cat heard a whooshing sound and saw a shadow overhead. Without stopping to think, he leaped off the bench and shot underneath it as the red-tailed hawk swooped down from the sky. With his wings spread wide, he was an awesome sight, majestic and intimidating.

The cat remained where he was, shaking with fear. He overheard a man shout to a woman, walking a small dog.

"Watch your pup, lady!" the man yelled. "I saw that hawk grab a squirrel the other day."

The woman scooped her scrawny Chihuahua up in her arms. As the tiny dog squawked with fright, the cat dove into a hole someone had dug beneath a fence. Heart pounding, he discovered the hole led into a tunnel. He crawled through and emerged on the other side of the fence, where he found refuge beneath a large tree.

He sat quietly for a minute or two, keeping his eyes closed as he tried to calm down. He thought peaceful thoughts. But he still found it hard to breathe. Even though he knew he was safe from the hawk's reach, he felt uncomfortable, as if he was being watched.

"You're being silly," he told himself, but his eyes flickered open, just to make sure.

To his horror, he saw three sets of eyes staring at him with suspicion. They belonged to three enormous dogs, sitting on a park bench a few feet away.

The cat was proud of how tough he could be. He got a kick out of provoking dogs by arching his back and hissing. He enjoyed watching them start to chase him and then get pulled up short by the leashes that attached them to their owners.

But these dogs weren't wearing leashes. He'd landed inside the dog run.

Worse than feeling scared, he felt defeated.

I can't run anymore, he thought, and shut his eyes, waiting to be crushed.

As he crouched, shuddering with fear, he heard a not-so-terrifying voice.

"Look who's over there," growled a sleek brown mutt with alert ears and dark eyes.

Her name was Maggie. She was a long-legged and muscular dog who wore a jaunty bandanna. Her brow was wrinkled, giving the impression she was puzzling through a complicated thought.

"That self-satisfied fat cat," sniffed her friend Roxie, an imposing brown beauty who didn't like snobs. "What's he doing in the dog run? What does he think? That he's the mayor of Washington Square?"

The cat sucked in his stomach.

"Fat! Me?" he thought, feeling a little insulted. For a second, his fear was overpowered by his vanity.

"Look at him," muttered Maggie, lowering her head so it wasn't obvious she was talking about the cat. "He's a mess. Maybe he's in trouble. Should we go ask him?"

The cat rubbed his ears with his paws. Had she said what he thought she said? He blinked and looked at Maggie's eyes. They seemed soft and friendly.

Just then, the third dog, a watchful fellow named Henry, offered a not-so-friendly observation.

"That cat is prowling around on his own," he said suspiciously. "Look! He isn't wearing a collar. I say it isn't any of our business. He got in here didn't he? Let him find his way out."

Maggie groaned, "How can you say that?" she asked. "He's in our neighborhood. Shouldn't we offer to help?"

Henry's face was thrust forward and his neck muscles were taut. He looked ready to pounce but held himself back. He had been working on controlling his temper. However, he couldn't hide his natural dislike for cats.

Roxie turned to Maggie and sighed.

"You, my dear are an incurable romantic," she said patiently. Roxie felt it was her duty to explain the way things worked to Maggie, who had moved to the city a few months earlier.

"This is New York City," Roxie said. "Neighborhoods change. Shops open and then they close. People move in and out. Nothing sits still."

Even though she knew Roxie meant well, Maggie hung her head. She was a sensitive type.

Roxie butted her friend with her head, her way of saying she didn't mean to sound snippy.

"I love incurable romantics," she said. "That's why we love you."

Maggie continued to mope.

Roxie knew how to put her friend into a better mood. Aware that Maggie couldn't resist a good romp, Roxie flung herself into a mix of gravel, leaves, and dirt piled up by a hole someone had dug next to the bench. As predicted, Maggie followed. The two friends wrestled a while, then stood up and shook themselves clean, though a few twigs remained stuck in the bright pink strap Roxie wore around her neck.

"Feel better?" Roxie said, catching her breath.

Still panting, Maggie dropped her jaw into a wide, toothy smile.

Roxie remembered the cat and stared at him.

He pretended to ignore her.

"He *is* a mess," she acknowledged, her voice softening.

A whistle sounded.

The cat watched all three dogs lift their heads in unison and race toward the entrance to the dog run. A handsome man was waiting for them, dangling their leashes. That was George, the dog walker, whose mere presence made them swoon. They sat looking up at him with adoration in their eyes.

As George attached leashes to their collars, Roxie glanced back. The cat looked so miserable Roxie couldn't stop herself.

"Come with us," she barked, nodding her head.

Henry started to object, but realized it was pointless to argue with Roxie. Maggie looked at her friend with admiration. Roxie didn't waste her breath on cheap pity. She took action.

George led his pack out of the dog run. He was unaware they were being trailed by a large mass of dirty white fur.

As they left the park, the cat glanced skyward, in time to see the hawk sailing toward the rooftops, with breakfast dangling from his mouth.

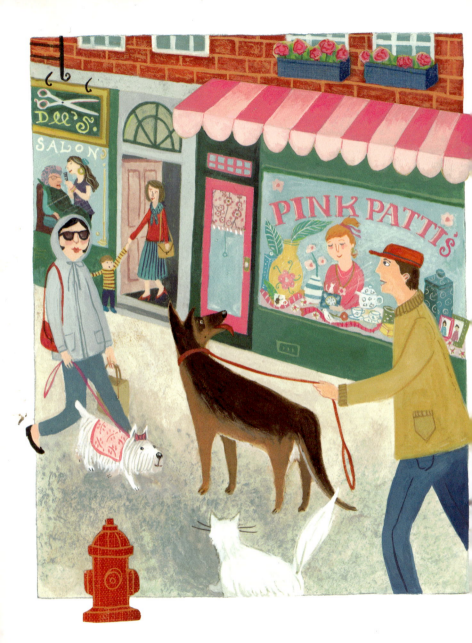

CHAPTER TWO

Pretty Boy

They dropped off Henry and then Maggie. The cat waited patiently while George took the dogs inside, hiding behind a fire hydrant so that the dog walker didn't notice him on the way out.

Finally they arrived at Roxie's stop, a store called Pink Patti's. Its bright pink awning seemed familiar to the cat, who had been roaming the Village streets for a few days. He might have stopped to check out his reflection in the window once (or twice), but hadn't bothered to peek inside.

Roxie turned her head toward the cat.

"This is where I get off," the dog said. "So long."

The cat was startled. Even though he was accustomed to traveling alone, he had enjoyed the comfort of the cozy pack.

As Roxie followed George inside, the cat raised his paw in salute and called out.

"Thanks!"

Roxie stuck her head out the door and barked. "See you around," she said.

The cat ambled off, fighting a vague feeling of disappointment. He told himself it had been a successful morning. He'd avoided being eaten by a hawk. He had made some interesting new acquaintances. What more could he ask for?

He shook himself from his shiny nose to the tip of his tail.

What he needed, he realized, was something to eat. He remembered spotting a café on the way from the park. After a wrong turn or two, he found the place, and congratulated himself for his astute sense of direction. He parked himself under a bench in front of the café, where people sat and sampled the snacks they'd bought. It didn't take long for him to collect a pile of satisfying scraps. After arranging them just so, he stuffed himself with gusto.

"I do love a nice piece of cheese," he said to himself, licking his lips as he swallowed a chunk of cheddar.

When his stomach was full, he felt better. He was not much of a planner but he was an optimist, the type of cat who always convinced himself he would land on his feet. He was also vain. He believed that appearance matters. Aware that his hair was his finest feature, he cleaned himself with his tongue. He fluffed his fur. He arranged his tail into a bouncy curve. Though he was still somewhat grimy, he felt refreshed.

With a light step, he turned the corner, feeling confident again. He wasn't surprised when a stylish woman coming his way knelt down to pet him with admiration in her eyes. He often had that effect on people.

"You are gorgeous," the woman said.

In response, the white cat purred and rubbed his head against her hand. He was so busy flirting, he failed to pay attention to her companion—a very large shaggy sheepdog.

While the cat preened, the dog bristled.

The cat pulled away, eyeing the dog nervously.

The woman laughed. "Don't be afraid of Poochie," she said. "He's a big softie."

Poochie growled as the woman kept on petting the cat.

"Don't be jealous, Poochie," the woman said.

The cat couldn't resist. He stuck out his tongue at the dog, while taunting him in a silky voice.

"Overgrown hairy beast," he purred.

That did it.

The big softie had a big fit.

Before the woman knew what was happening, Poochie lunged and the cat skedaddled.

The woman was so startled she dropped the dog's leash. Off he went, ignoring her cries of "Stop!"

The cat zoomed and zigzagged until he ended up back in front of the shop with the pink awning. Even

though the sheepdog was closing in on him, he stopped. He had to catch his breath.

A brief observation passed through his mind as he gasped for air.

"Maybe I *am* getting fat," he thought.

Poochie was huffing and puffing, too, but showed no signs of slowing down. At wit's end, the cat let out a wail that sounded like a desperate baby.

Once again, Roxie came to his rescue.

As if she'd been waiting for him, she pushed open the door with her head. The cat scooted beneath her legs, to safety, as Poochie was about to catch up with him. The dog planted himself outside and pressed his large head against the door window, glaring.

He found himself staring eye to eye with Roxie's fiercest face.

That was enough for Poochie. He was transformed from scary to softie in an instant. Whimpering, he trotted away and sat at his owner's feet, sweet as he could be.

Roxie sniffed as she heard the woman say, "You silly puppy, what got into you? You know I love you better than any old cat!"

"Ridiculous!" Roxie huffed. "What a spoiled brat."

The cat nodded weakly. As he lay wheezing on the floor, he heard someone calling out from another room.

"What's all the commotion?"

The voice was light and springy.

That was the cat's introduction to Patti, the human who lived with Roxie.

Then she appeared. The cat could never tell how old humans were by looking at them, but he suspected she wasn't as young as she sounded. Her reddish hair was pulled on top of her head in a wayward ponytail. Her eyes were small and sparkly. Her clothes were dramatic—a brightly colored sweater pulled over a long pleated skirt.

The cat immediately liked her. He was always drawn to artistic types, and Patti was a work of art.

When she saw the cat huddled on the floor underneath Roxie's legs, she burst out laughing. "Look what the dog dragged in!" she said, and laughed again.

"That's Patti," Roxie whispered to the cat, "This is her shop. She loves to be silly but don't be fooled. She's the wisest person I know."

The cat saw that Roxie loved Patti and sensed that he might come to feel the same way.

Patti was a polite hostess. "You must be thirsty," she said to the panting cat.

She disappeared through a doorway, giving the cat time to look around. He tiptoed carefully, keeping a respectful distance from the shelves filled with whimsical teacups, embroidered pillows, colorful notebooks, unusual jewelry, and clever little boxes.

"What kind of store is this?" the cat asked Roxie.

Roxie didn't answer right away. She liked to be precise.

"Patti has been through a lot," she said, trying to explain without being a gossip. "But she never complains. She always says her main talent is her ability to remember happiness as well as sadness. That's what she sells. Things that help people remember."

The cat listened to Patti whistling as she clattered around in the next room.

"Why is it called Pink Patti's?" he asked.

"That's easy," said Roxie. "She traveled to Japan when she was young and fell in love . . . with cherry blossoms, among other things. The flowers reminded her of her romance. Neither of them lasted long, but both were beautiful and left few regrets. After that she liked wearing pink. A friend called her Pink Patti and it stuck."

Roxie lifted her head so the cat could get a better look at the pink ribbon around her neck. He could see it was embossed with flowers.

"She calls this her cherry blossom ribbon," Roxie said. "She wraps everything in it."

The cat was about to reply when Patti returned with a saucer of milk.

As she knelt down to put the saucer on the floor, she asked, with a grin, "What are the two of you conspiring about?"

They knew she didn't really expect an answer.

While the cat lapped up some milk, Patti scratched Roxie behind the ears and thought. After several minutes, she popped up and strode over to the front door.

"C'mon, pretty boy," she said, looking at the cat. "Time to go."

The cat hung his head.

"Why is she kicking me out already?" he muttered with a low meow.

Roxie heard him.

"Don't worry," she said to her new friend. "Patti wouldn't do that. She has empathy to spare."

"Empathy?" The cat didn't know what that meant.

Roxie explained. "It means she understands what's going on inside—that goes for humans and animals."

The cat was convinced when he heard Patti say, "Don't worry." Her voice was so calm and reassuring it was easy to trust her.

The cat walked toward her.

"Roxie, watch the shop for a few minutes," Patti called out as she led the cat next door to another store.

It was a hair salon.

"Hey, Dee," Patti called out. "I have a new customer for you."

Dee, the owner, waved a pair of scissors. She was tall and angular, with a long mane of dark brown hair accented with light streaks.

"I'll be over in a minute," she said, then returned to her clipping.

The cat stared intently at Dee as she worked. He observed that the hairstylist was a good talker and a good listener, a combination that was not all that common. Most people tend to be one or the other.

Patti sat and picked up a magazine while the cat curled up at her feet. He raised his head and looked around. He saw a couple of old ladies with curlers in their hair, chatting with the young man in a business suit, whose hair was being trimmed. Next to him sat a girl with many tattoos and a metal stud in her right eyebrow, waiting for the dye in her hair to set.

At Dee's, he noticed all kinds of characters seemed to feel at home.

"What's his name?" Dee asked, looking at the cat.

Patti looked puzzled. "I don't know," she said. "Let me think about it."

She thought for quite a while.

The cat was impatient to hear what she would suggest. He'd been called quite a few names in his day, but none of them had ever stuck. Maybe because he'd never stayed around anywhere long enough for a name to seem like it belonged to him.

He liked the fact that Patti was taking her time. It made him feel important. After what seemed like forever, she said, "I've got it!"

The cat's eyes widened.

Patti picked up him.

"How about Pretty Boy?" she asked.

He blinked in approval.

A perfect name for a good-looking guy, he thought.

Dee raised her eyebrows and shook her head.

"Not yet," she said as she yanked the cat out of Patti's arms.

Before he could object, the cat was doused in water and scrubbed with soap. Before he could yowl his objection, he was blasted with warm air.

Dee laughed as she completed the wash and blow-dry with a brisk comb out.

"*Now*," said Dee to the bewildered cat, "you are Pretty Boy."

The cat stopped cowering. After a quick glance in the mirror, he stretched and tossed his head back, with the self-assurance of a movie star.

"What a knockout!" said one of the old ladies.

The girl with the tattoos took a look.

"Cool," she said.

Dee smiled with self-satisfaction and then frowned when she noticed the way Patti was looking back and forth between her and the cat.

"Oh, no!" Dee said. "No pets for me. It's great to have Roxie come for a visit now and then. But I don't need more than that."

Patti didn't say a word.

"No!" said Dee.

Pretty Boy sat still, occasionally giving his freshly coiffed tail a dramatic wave.

Dee continued.

"I loved my cats when I was little, but we had a big house with a yard," she said. "I swore I'd never have a pet in the city."

Patti let her go on.

"Besides," said Dee, "I've reached a point in my life where I like being unattached. I can come and go as I please."

Patti kept nodding in silence, her lips pressed together like she was trying to hold back a secret. All the while, she noticed that Dee couldn't take her eyes off Pretty Boy. She couldn't help herself from grinning when she saw him admiring himself in the mirror.

"He really does look elegant," she said.

Dee picked Pretty Boy up and talked directly to him.

"Okay, buster," she said. "Here's the deal. You can't live here but I'll keep food and water for you inside the door. You can drop by anytime you want."

When he rubbed his head against her hand, she put him back on the floor.

"For a visit!" she warned.

Patti was beaming as she said, "Hey, Dee, I've got to go. Roxie's alone in the store!"

Before Dee could protest, Patti had disappeared out the front door.

Dee looked down at Pretty Boy and sighed.

So Pretty Boy and Dee began the kind of relation-ship that was common in the city. They depended on each other up to a point, but didn't go so far as to admit there was an obligation. Dee didn't invite Pretty Boy to live with her, but she did keep her promise. She always kept a fresh bowl of food and another filled with water at the ready. On days when Pretty Boy didn't show up, Dee felt a pang of emptiness. After she arrived at the shop one rainy day to find Pretty Boy waiting, shivering, and miserable, she bought a litter box which she kept in the back. From then on, when the weather was unpleasant, Pretty Boy had a place to stay.

CHAPTER THREE

Friends

Pretty Boy realized he had become part of the group when George the dog walker started stopping by Dee's to see if the cat was going to join him and the dogs. Occasionally, outside on the street, people would do a double take when they saw the three dogs on leashes trailed by a handsome white cat. But in Washington Square, no one batted an eye. There were much stranger things to see there. Like the guy who walked around with a giant bird sitting on his head. Or the man who wheeled his piano into the park almost every day and played concerts that went on for hours, even when it was so cold he had to wear gloves.

Compared with them, a dog pack plus one cat was not that noteworthy.

Except that Pretty Boy found his new situation rather extraordinary. After spending so much time as a loner, he was learning to become a friend.

It wasn't always easy. He was amazed to discover how much dogs enjoyed small talk. Even grumpy Henry could devote large amounts of time commenting on what was happening around them.

For example:

"Can you believe that collar?" Roxie said, when a new dog came to the park wearing a strap studded with fake jewels.

"What's wrong with it?" Maggie responded.

"Everything?" Henry added.

This exchange caused them to collapse in a fit of barking laughter.

If George decided they'd been sitting too long and threw a stick across the dog run, the three of them would stop in the middle of a sentence and chase it, without a backward glance.

There were times when Pretty Boy was annoyed by their inability to stay focused. There were moments he found their conversation petty and inane. But over time he found himself chiming in.

He drew the line, however, at chasing sticks. This he simply would not do, no matter how many times Roxie teased him by waving a twig right in front of him.

"It's strange enough for me to pal around with a pack of dogs," he would say to her. "If I start chasing sticks today, what'll it be tomorrow? Barking? No thanks!"

Roxie responded by vigorously waving the piece of wood clamped between her teeth in Pretty Boy's face before burying it under a bench.

"You don't know what you're missing," she would say to him in a way that made him curious. But not so curious that he began to chase sticks.

Friendship didn't happen overnight. It took time for Pretty Boy to learn that Maggie lived with a boy named Eli and a girl named Lilly, and that Henry had been to anger management classes. It took even longer for Pretty Boy to accept Roxie's generosity. That wasn't easy for him. Nor was it easy for him to trust the humans. He had learned self-reliance the hard way.

CHAPTER FOUR

Low Notes
and High Ones

S everal weeks passed before Pretty Boy allowed himself to admit that he felt comfortable at Dee's. Then he worried he might be too comfortable.

His dog friends knew things had changed when Pretty Boy started telling them stories about Dee and talking about the hair salon as if it belonged to him, too.

"We're a good team," he observed one day. "I'm like Dee in that I know how to satisfy a customer. When I see someone who is allergic to cats, or just doesn't like us, I hide under the counter or go out for a walk. If I see that someone needs extra attention, I snuggle at her feet while Dee washes her hair."

When Roxie heard this she whispered to Maggie, "He might be vain but he does seem to have a talent. He can spot loneliness without even looking."

Maggie turned an affectionate gaze on Pretty Boy. Because she had been the first dog to accept him, she felt as though his successes were hers.

Roxie had heard from Patti and Dee that Pretty Boy was a disappointment in one way.

"Catch any mice at the shop?" she teased.

"I'm not that kind of cat," Pretty Boy said haughtily. "I have no interest in chasing rodents."

Henry guffawed.

"Sounds like you're scared to me," he barked.

"That's ridiculous!" said Pretty Boy, covering his embarrassment with indignation. "I simply don't want to be around creatures that carry disease."

"Hmmph," said Henry. "I think you're a germaphobe!"

"Germaphobe?!!" exclaimed Roxie. "My, my. Aren't you the fancy-pants!"

Maggie intervened. "Henry, Roxie, stop it!"

Before Henry could reply a fight broke out across the dog park, diverting his attention. He restrained himself from running to join the hubbub, but barked at the top of his lungs. By the time Henry settled down, Pretty Boy was perched on a bench enjoying the sun. The subject of mice was forgotten.

That afternoon, as they often did, Pretty Boy and Dee met Roxie and Patti after work at an outdoor café. The dog and cat sat under the table, listening to the women talk.

Roxie sighed with pleasure. "Don't you love all their theories and opinions?" she said to Pretty Boy.

He responded with a stretch of happiness.

A mild winter came and went and then it was spring again. To his delight, Pretty Boy discovered the cherry blossoms flowering in Washington Square. Thanks to Pink Patti, he now could identify what they were. This knowledge made him admire them even more. They became individuals, not part of the crowd. It was like him having a name—another gift from Patti.

When the fragile flowers began falling softly like snow, he deliberately stood beneath the trees, hoping the petals might land on him as they fluttered to the ground. Remembering the story Roxie had told him about Pink Patti's love of cherry blossoms, he wanted to arrive at her shop covered in the flowers.

When Patti saw the fluffy white cat adorned with pink blossoms, she burst into a strange combination of laughing and crying.

"Pretty Boy, you are quite a character," she said as she brushed the petals off his fur.

She began to recite a poem by Ueshima Onitsura, a Japanese poet she loved.

"They blossom, and then we gaze, and then the blooms scatter," she said, giving Pretty Boy a tight hug.

He was unaware that Patti's tears were not simply her way of saying thank you.

He didn't know how to read, so he hadn't paid attention to the signs that had been appearing all over the neighborhood.

STORE FOR RENT

He didn't even notice when one of those signs appeared right next to Pink Patti's shop, above the storefront window, way above his eye level.

Then, lying at Dee's feet one day, enjoying the sun as the women sipped drinks at their favorite café, he overheard the following conversation:

"I don't know how much longer I can hang on to the store," Patti said. "Everyone but my landlord seems to know that people don't have as much money to spend as they used to. He's raising the rent."

"What a jerk," Dee said.

"But don't worry," she added. "You'll manage. People love coming to Pink Patti's."

Her tone didn't match her reassuring words.

Pretty Boy's ears opened wide as he tried to comprehend what he was hearing.

"They may love to come in but that doesn't mean they can afford to buy things," Patti said. "I may have to leave."

Pretty Boy's reaction was instant and unplanned, like a sneeze or a shiver. He began to run, trying to put distance between himself and those awful words. Ignoring

Roxie's barks, he raced down the block and into the street, where a taxi skidded sideways to avoid hitting him. He ran through a puddle and shuddered as dirty water splashed on him. He ran and ran until he ended up in Washington Square. He collapsed by the fountain.

Flat on his back, gasping for breath, he saw the red-tailed hawk circling above.

Just come get me, Pretty Boy thought, closing his eyes.

But his survival instinct was stronger than his despair. He forced himself to open his eyes and prepare to scamper, if necessary.

Nothing happened.

The hawk must have already eaten or had other things on his mind.

Pretty Boy had to admit he felt relieved, even as he sank into feelings of gloom and frustration. Patti had rescued him from the streets and taught him so much. She had recognized that he was not a mere alley cat but Pretty Boy, a cat of consequence. Yet he could do nothing for her when she needed help. He was a useless creature!

If Patti left, Roxie would go with her. And without Roxie, where would he be?

Wasn't there anything that he could do for them?

Crouched in the ground, he was about to sink into a swamp of self-pity, when he was stopped by a haunting melody. All at once he was forced to pay attention to something besides the despair swelling within.

Pretty Boy lifted his head. What was this music? It sounded as sad as he felt. He got up and began walking toward the mesmerizing sound.

He didn't have to go far. Under the Arch he found a man sitting on a stool, his left hand placed on the neck of a large, beautiful instrument made of dark wood. Both the man and his cello were etched with the lines of time. A small audience gathered around him.

The Cello Man was slender, wearing a cotton sweater over a white shirt. His collar was pressed. He was very neat, except for the strands of white hair flying loose from the beret on his head. Even as his fingers flew up and down the instrument's strings, his body remained still.

As Pretty Boy watched and listened, he felt calm again, as though someone had flipped a switch inside him, lighting up a dark place. He didn't understand how, but that sad music made him feel better.

The comforting feeling lingered after the music stopped.

"What were you playing?" someone asked.

The Cello Man answered, "The Suites for Cello by Johann Sebastian Bach."

"When did he compose them?"

"Ages ago," the Cello Man said. "In the seventeen hundreds."

Pretty Boy didn't have a good sense of time. But he understood this music was ancient. He was impressed that something created by a man so long ago could feel like it was written for him. It made him feel part of something much bigger than himself.

His internal philosophizing was interrupted by a familiar bark.

His friend Maggie had been listening, too. Pretty Boy had been so absorbed he hadn't noticed her, even though she was wearing a bright red bandanna. She was a few feet away, next to a small boy and a smaller girl, who was asleep in a stroller she appeared to have out-grown.

That must be Eli and Lilly, Pretty Boy thought. Eli was the seven-year-old boy who was Maggie's official owner. Lilly was his little sister. Pretty Boy had heard all about them from Maggie, but this was the first time he'd actually seen them. They were always in school when

Maggie joined the dogs for walks with George. The cat concluded that the woman with them must be their mother.

Maggie had been sitting patiently, waiting for the music to stop. She was torn between her urge to let Pretty Boy know she was there and her desire to please Eli, who had commanded her to sit quietly. This act of restraint took all Maggie's willpower. It was especially admirable because loud noises made her nervous. But she didn't mind the sounds coming out of the cello. She found them soothing. This made it easier for her to behave like a "good dog."

Pretty Boy raised his paw in greeting, and then the Cello Man began to play again. Pretty Boy felt wistful as he watched Eli slip his hand into his mother's while they listened. The cat had been a kitten when he'd been separated from his mother. He had been on his own ever since.

As the cello's music soared and whispered, danced and wept, Pretty Boy felt as though he and his fellow listeners had been transported to a secret space. The surrounding noises of the park seemed to disappear. There were no barks, squeals, honks, or chatter within this invisible boundary, marked by music.

Pretty Boy became aware that Eli was watching him. The boy whispered to his mother, "Look at that cat! His tail is keeping time with the music."

Pretty Boy's head snapped around to look. It was true! He hadn't even noticed.

But the Cello Man had.

When he took a break, he laughed and pointed at him.

"I don't need a metronome with that cat around."

Then he said to Eli's mother. "Does your son play an instrument?" he asked. "He seems to have a strong connection to music."

When she shook her head no, the musician turned to Eli. "Have you ever thought about lessons?" he asked.

The boy looked surprised. With a grin on his face, he walked next to the cello, which was much taller than he was. He touched the wood with his little hand, which had the texture of a fresh peach.

"How could that be?" he asked. He sounded very serious, like someone much older than he was.

The Cello Man laughed.

"You'd have to start small," he said. "They make little cellos."

Eli's mother bought one of the CDs neatly displayed

in the Cello Man's open case. The old man gathered up the rest and placed them in a shopping bag. He put the cello away, hoisted the case onto his back. As he left the park he nodded at Pretty Boy and waved to Eli.

Maggie barked good-bye to Pretty Boy, who decided to stroll around the park before going home. Dusk was about to fall. Pretty Boy loved this magic hour when evening crept in and the sky glowed pink. As he walked home, he replayed the music in his head and tried to think of a way to help his friends.

CHAPTER FIVE

Eli

Maggie noticed on the way home from the park that Eli was in a much better mood than he had been for a long time. Things had changed a lot since they had to move to New York. Everything was different in the city. Instead of living in a house with a yard where Maggie could play, they squeezed into an apartment.

Maggie didn't mind. In fact, she was happier than she had been. She had more friends now than before. She enjoyed her daily excursions to the park with George.

Lilly had adjusted easily. She had started nursery school and returned home every day full of stories of her new adventures.

Eli, however, had become quiet and grouchy. Maggie had gotten used to his complaints: The streets were too busy. It was too noisy. Nothing was ever the same one day to the next.

Occasionally she heard a note of grudging excitement in his voice—like when giant trailers parked on curbs near their house. This meant a movie or TV show was being filmed. He heard someone explain why. Apparently, his neighborhood was "picturesque"—a word he thought meant old and crowded until his parents explained it meant "charming."

Mostly, however, Eli did not find it charming. And the rats! They were everywhere—in the subway, on the streets, in the parks. They were definitely NOT charming or picturesque.

Maggie hurt for him. She saw that he felt out of place everywhere he went. He liked school as well as you could without having any real friends. His teacher was nice and he got along with the other kids, but mostly he felt alone.

He complained to Maggie at night, when they were by themselves in his room.

"My parents don't understand," he told her. "They see me playing soccer and doing homework and going to the playground and figure everything is okay. And when I tell them I'm unhappy they just ask a lot of questions."

Maggie gazed at him sympathetically.

Eli mimicked his parents.

"Did something happen at school?"

"Was somebody mean to you?"

"What can we do to make it better?"

"The trouble is," he said to himself and his dog, "I don't know what to tell them. It's not like anything *happened* or that someone was *mean*."

Tears leaked out of the corners of his eyes.

Maggie looked distressed.

"Make it like it was before," he said, pounding his pillow.

He planted his head facedown on the mattress. Maggie placed her paw on his back, but not even this friendly gesture seemed to help.

Last week, however, she overheard Eli tell his parents he had discovered there was something he did like about the city.

"You never know what sounds you are going to hear," he said enthusiastically. "It's pretty cool to find someone playing the drums in a subway station. Or those guys we saw in the subway playing in a band while the train was rocking back and forth. I kept waiting for them to fall over but they didn't!"

So Maggie wasn't surprised that today, when Eli heard the Cello Man's music wafting across Washington Square Park, he pulled all of them over to listen. By the

time Pretty Boy saw them there, they had been listening for a very long time. The boy seemed rooted to the pavement.

When they got home that evening, he seemed excited about school for the first time since they'd moved to New York.

Once a week, after lunch, the teacher asked one student to show the class something that represented who they were. Eli had been dreading his turn. Months had gone by and almost everyone in the class but him had presented at "share."

Now he had something he wanted to take in. Before bed he listened to the Cello Man's CD from beginning to end and thought about what he wanted to say about it. He packed the CD into his lunch bag so he wouldn't forget it. For the first time in a long while, he slept with a smile on his face, dreaming of tomorrow and how great things were going to be.

CHAPTER SIX

Maggie Tells What Happened Next

Pretty Boy was in fine spirits the following afternoon when George picked Roxie and him up for an outing to the park. Maggie and Henry were with them, as usual.

But Maggie was agitated.

"Poor Eli," she began, after they arrived at the dog run and huddled in their favorite spot.

Her friends listened as she told them what had happened when Eli took the cello music to school for "share."

The morning had passed very slowly, Maggie told them, as Eli mentally practiced his presentation. He couldn't wait to see how excited his classmates were going to be when he played the CD.

"After lunch his teacher, Ms. Jodi, called him to the front of the room," said Maggie. "She helped him put the CD into the player. Before he pressed the *play* button, Eli told the class about how he first heard the music. He explained what a cello looked like, drawing a picture with his hands, the way his dad had suggested. They smiled when he told them about the old man's cool beret, and how even his dog, Maggie, liked the music."

Maggie paused and lowered her head in a little bow, to the amusement of her friends.

Then she resumed the story.

"They laughed when he described the cat whose tail kept time with the music."

Now it was Pretty Boy's turn to look pleased with himself.

Maggie continued.

"Things were going very well," she said. "He decided it was time to push the *play* button. He stood there watching his classmates, filled with excitement as the sounds of the Cello Man began."

Maggie told the story very dramatically from her perch on the bench. She growled, to let her friends know something awful was about to happen.

"Then he noticed something disturbing," she said. "None of them seemed to be paying attention. Even Billy, who is on his soccer team and is kind of a friend, was doodling on a piece of paper. Some girls were whispering.

"Eli knew Ms. Jodi saw him clamp his lips together so he wouldn't cry."

"Listen to this beautiful music," she said to the class.

"I don't get it," a boy called out.

"Me neither," said another.

Maggie saw her audience was hooked.

"Eli's cheeks got red, and he felt his lunch rising from his stomach into his throat," she said, rather poetically. "He wished he could disappear. He wanted to get it over with but refused to cut off the music. He waited until the song was over before he pressed *stop*.

"That evening he told us the story and said to his parents, 'The kids in my class are idiots.' And then he said, 'I don't want to be a weirdo.'"

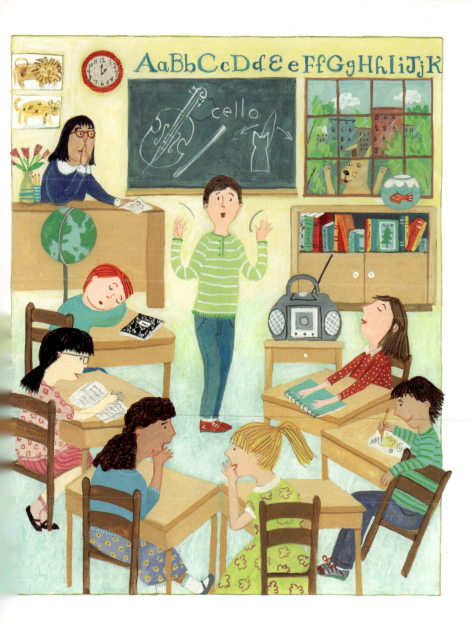

Maggie looked upset, but pressed on with the story.

"You could tell his mother wanted to say, 'Yes they are idiots,' and 'No you aren't a weirdo.'"

Maggie sighed and paused.

Roxie grew impatient. "Well, what *did* she say?"

Maggie collected herself.

"She said, 'People have different tastes in music. It's their loss.' But I knew that even as she said the words, she knew how awful he must feel."

Pretty Boy meowed in sympathy.

"I knew how upset Eli was when I watched him toss the Cello Man's CD into the trash basket by his bed," Maggie said. "I knew this was a mistake but didn't know how to explain it to the boy. When he went to the bathroom to brush his teeth, I stuck my head in the

basket and pulled the CD out carefully with my teeth, trying not to scratch it."

"Go girl," said Roxie with admiration.

"I looked around the room for a place to hide it. There wasn't much time! After I heard Eli come out of the bathroom, I nudged open his closet door and slipped the CD under a pile of clothes at the bottom!"

The animals erupted into a chorus of approval.

Maggie went on. "When Eli returned to his room and climbed into bed, I took my usual place next to his feet.

"Then he scratched my head with his toes and muttered, 'I hate it here,' right before he sank into sleep."

The animals sat silently for several minutes. Maggie had given them a big story to digest.

Pretty Boy understood how Eli felt. The cat knew what it was like to feel rejected. But now, thanks to Patti and his new friends, he'd also come to understand what it felt like to be accepted.

As Maggie told her story, Pretty Boy realized something important about himself. He didn't know how to read, but he was quick-witted. He knew how to survive. But he also knew he wanted more. He needed love and music and the crazy mix of creatures (except rats) he found every day on the streets of New York. He hadn't yet found his talent, but he knew he had an artist's soul. Maybe he could help the boy find his.

He didn't say all of that to his friends. Instead, before he realized he'd opened his mouth, he said to Maggie, "He shouldn't give up on music!"

Roxie chimed in. "I had the same thought."

Pretty Boy mused, "Maybe he should take cello lessons, like the old man suggested."

Before they could discuss this further, George called out, "What's with you dogs? It's a beautiful day and you're sitting around. Go run!"

For extra incentive, he tossed a ball across the dog run.

Pretty Boy remained in place as his friends raced away. No matter how many times he witnessed their absolute obedience to George, it never failed to impress him. The cat couldn't imagine what it was like to have that kind of blind devotion to anyone. None of his canine friends had been able to explain it to him in a way that made sense.

Pretty Boy didn't want to be judgmental, but he thought it was a little undignified.

Henry reached the ball first and grabbed it in his powerful jaws. He ran back to George and dropped the ball at the dog walker's feet.

"One question," Henry huffed, looking in Pretty Boy's direction, while trying to catch his breath. "How are you going to convince Eli?"

CHAPTER SEVEN

Trapped

The next day Roxie arrived at Dee's carrying a small bag in her teeth.

Dee let the dog in and pulled out the note that was sticking out of the bag. She read it and smiled.

"Pretty Boy, this is a present for you from Patti," she said. "Apparently, it's your anniversary."

He replied with a puzzled look.

"It's been six months since you showed up at Patti's door," Dee explained, reading the note again.

"Shall I open the box?" Dee asked.

Without waiting for Pretty Boy to answer, she pulled off the pink ribbon, pried open the cardboard lid, and pulled out a handsome black collar made of velvet. She held it up and inspected the metal tag hanging from it.

"Look at this," she said with delight.

Pretty Boy obeyed. He saw that the metal was engraved with little blossoms and some words.

"That Patti," said Dee, shaking her head. "She's amazing."

"Pretty Boy, here's your name."

She pointed.

"And here's my telephone number."

She pointed again.

She read the card Patti wrote for Pretty Boy out loud.

"'Dearest Pretty Boy,'" the card began. "'Thank you for showing up at our doorstep six months ago. You have been a fine addition to our little block. But when I watched you and Roxie hanging out the other day I realized something was missing. You don't have a collar! I always want you to be able to find your way home. So I made you this one. It's got cherry blossoms like Roxie's to remind you of her—and me! And the black velvet seemed so dashing—like you!!!!!'"

Dee slipped the collar around Pretty Boy's neck. Patti had been right. The black strap looked striking against his white fur.

Pretty Boy jumped up on a chair and admired himself in one of the salon mirrors. With a collar like that he felt ready to take on the world. He would find a way to save Patti's shop! He would help Eli find happiness!

Then summer came. The higher the temperature rose, the lower Pretty Boy's energy fell. He found it impossible to concentrate. His good intentions regarding Patti's problems and Eli's musical education melted in the heat. All he wanted to do was sleep.

One sultry morning Roxie convinced him to walk to Washington Square with her and George and the other dogs. "You can take a nap once we get there," she said.

"Besides," she added slyly, "if you lay around you are going to get completely out of shape."

What did she mean, completely *out of shape?* Pretty Boy thought indignantly. *I'm in excellent shape!*

But when he glanced at his belly, he couldn't deny it was even rounder than it had been. This disturbed him. He did not want to let himself go. He admired himself too much for that! With a grumbling sound, he pulled himself to his feet and trotted briskly after the dogs, glaring at Roxie all the while. Why did she have to be so smart?

By the time they reached the dog run, he was ready for the promised nap. He rested a long time.

He hated the heat. No matter how much he slept, he was still tired. He could barely keep up with George and the pack on the way home. As usual, Pretty Boy waited outside while George took the dogs inside to drop off Maggie. The air was so heavy that Pretty Boy fell into a daydream the instant the door closed behind them. He couldn't keep his eyes open, not knowing he was about to get the whammy of a lifetime:

Quick and dangerous as a summer storm, a biker in a hurry turned tranquility into chaos. Without warning, he ran over Pretty Boy's tail. The shock sent the dozing cat up into the air, screeching with pain and indignation. He was flying, waving his paws every which way— until gravity yanked him back to the sidewalk.

He landed with a thud.

Pretty Boy lay still for a minute, blinking at the sun's glare. All he wanted was a shady place to recover.

Then he noticed an open car trunk, right next to him at the curb. Pretty Boy hopped in, curled up behind a duffel bag, and immediately fell asleep.

He dimly heard Roxie barking anxiously and George's voice asking, "Where did Pretty Boy go?"

The poor cat was too dazed by all that had happened to muster a meow. He barely stirred when someone slammed the trunk door shut. Pretty Boy was trapped and he didn't even know it.

CHAPTER EIGHT

The Unexpected Journey

When Pretty Boy next opened his eyes, he had no idea where he was or how long he'd been there. The darkness that had been so inviting now was ominous.

Pretty Boy tried to move, but found that he was wedged in by heavy objects. Still stunned by his mis-adventure, he whimpered. Everything hurt. He thought he heard voices and a slamming noise, but he was too groggy to budge. He sank back into a deep sleep.

He didn't know how long he was out. When he woke up, he tried to look around but he couldn't see a thing.

Pretty Boy opened his mouth and screeched and bawled. But it was no use. No one responded.

He felt as if the ground was moving beneath him.

What was happening?

He was about to start wailing again when he heard a familiar sound in his head. The Cello Man's music blew over him like a comforting breeze. He could breathe again.

He was amazed at the power of his memory. The music felt real. He was also impressed by his ability to recall every note of so many complicated pieces. *Not only am I beautiful,* Pretty Boy thought, as he puffed out his chest, *I must be a genius.*

Hadn't the Cello Man said as much, when Eli pointed out Pretty Boy's ability to keep time with his tail?

These thoughts floated through Pretty Boy's mind as the music continued. In fact, he was now hearing songs in his head that he could swear he had never heard before.

The mind is a miraculous thing, he thought as he relaxed and listened and waited.

He was surprised at how calm he felt.

He had become so calm that everything seemed to slow down. The music got louder.

There was a small jolt, followed by silence. Pretty Boy shivered, light came flooding in.

CHAPTER NINE

The Best-Laid Plans

Pretty Boy heard a shriek and then a woman's voice. "I can't believe this!" she said. "Look what's in the trunk."

Pretty Boy was stunned. He lay where he was. He blinked into the light and tried to focus on the shadows dancing in front of him.

He was assaulted by a barrage of noises. A man was laughing, some children were shouting, a dog was barking.

The barking grew louder.

It was joined by the high voice of a little girl, who sounded delighted.

"What a pretty cat!" she called out.

"Lilly, calm down," a boy said. "You've seen cats before. Maggie, stop barking!"

Pretty Boy was confused. Maggie? Was it *his* Maggie? The bark did sound familiar.

He squinted. The boy was familiar, too.

Eli?

"What is going on?" he meowed.

Maggie was beside herself when she recognized her friend. She barked so furiously she could barely breathe.

"Pretty Boy," panted Maggie. "How did you end up in our car?"

"What car?" replied Pretty Boy as he struggled to climb over the packages that were piled in the trunk.

The boy laughed as he watched the cat meow and the dog bark in response.

"Mom," he shouted. "That's the cat from Washington Square. Remember? The one with the metronome tail."

His mother stood in front of the open trunk, shaking her head.

While she and Eli's father talked, Pretty Boy told Maggie about his tail getting run over by the bike and his leap into the unknown.

"Where are we?" he asked the dog.

"We're on our way to Maine," said Maggie. "That's where the kids' grandmother lives. We go there every summer for a couple of weeks."

"Kids?" asked Pretty Boy.

"Eli and his little sister, Lilly."

"I didn't know he had a sister," Pretty Boy said.

"You never pay attention!" Maggie replied. "She was asleep in the stroller when you met Eli in the park. And I've told you about her!"

Pretty Boy finished wiggling out from the suitcase trap and sat on top of one of them.

He started to say, "Yes, I do pay attention," but then decided this wasn't the time to argue.

"Where are we at this moment?" he asked, making an effort to appear calm.

Maggie looked around.

"At a rest stop," she said. "The kids had to go to the bathroom. So do I."

She ran off to the grass by the side of the parking lot.

Eli's mom and dad walked over to Pretty Boy.

"Well, kitty, this is a situation," said Eli's mom as she scratched Pretty Boy behind the ears.

"Look!" she called out to Eli's dad.

She held the tag hanging around Pretty Boy's neck between her fingers and read the inscription.

"You must be Pretty Boy," she laughed.

"Here's a phone number."

While Eli's dad took the kids to the bathroom, Eli's mom made a telephone call.

Pretty Boy sat and listened.

"This is going to sound strange, but we have your cat," Eli's mom began.

Pretty Boy understood Dee was on the other end. He wished he could hear her side of the conversation. He could only imagine her surprise. He wondered if she was worried.

He called out, to let her know he was all right.

Eli's mom laughed.

"I think Pretty Boy is saying hello," she said.

Then she explained that they were about five hours away from the city, north of Boston, and still had five hours to go.

She said they were planning to be at her mother's house in the country for two weeks.

She said this and that and listened as Dee said this and that.

When the conversation ended, she knelt down by Pretty Boy.

"Well, sir," she said. "You are taking a vacation in Maine."

Pretty Boy didn't know what to think. "Vacation" and "Maine" were just words to him, but they sounded good. He felt safe and even a little excited.

As they drove off, cello music filled the car.

Pretty Boy looked startled. How had the music in his head escaped?

Maggie noticed his perplexed expression.

"Remember how I told you I rescued the Cello Man's CD from Eli's trash can?" she asked. "When his mom was packing for the trip she found it in his closet. When we were in the car, she started playing it. You should have seen the look on Eli's face! But he didn't say a word. And when it reached the end, he asked her if she would play it again. Just like that."

Pretty Boy felt as pleased as if he'd rescued the Cello Man's music himself. Mainly he was relieved. How quickly things change. Instead of being trapped in a dark nowhere, he was now riding in comfort on the way to Maine, wherever that was.

And, he noticed, he had acquired a new admirer.

"I love this cat," declared Lilly, who was four years old. She was pale and freckled, with light brown hair, some of which was squeezed into pigtails while the rest flew here and there.

She sneezed.

"I hope you aren't catching a cold," said her mom as they settled in for another long drive.

They drove and drove until Eli's dad exclaimed: "We have now entered the great state of Maine."

Pretty Boy smiled to himself as he remembered hearing someone recite a famous line, written by the Scottish poet Robert Burns. "The best-laid schemes of mice and men/Often go awry."

But sometimes, Pretty Boy said to himself, the not-very-well-thought-out accidents that happen to cats and dogs work out surprisingly well.

CHAPTER TEN

Where Time Stands Still

They arrived at the house in Maine well past midnight. Eli and Lilly's mom and dad carried their sleepy children inside.

"Where are we?" Lilly asked in a dreamy voice.

"Go back to sleep," her mom said, kissing her on the forehead. "We're at Grandma's house. She already went to bed. We'll see her in the morning."

Maggie ran with excitement to all corners of the house and then planted herself on a crocheted rug, outside the children's room.

Pretty Boy watched Maggie become a furry lump.

Eli and Lilly's mom dropped a small blanket on the floor next to the dog, who was motionless, except for the rise and fall of her chest.

"Here, Pretty Boy," the children's mom said. "You can use this as a bed. Welcome to Paradise."

Turning to their dad, she said, "Let's unpack in the morning."

The grown-ups disappeared up the stairs.

Pretty Boy was so tired he didn't bother to look around. He fell asleep right away, even though the air was bracing, even chilly. His last thought for the night was: *I wonder what Paradise will look like.*

Soon enough he discovered what it *sounded* like.

He was awakened in the middle of the night to a terrifying symphony of noises. He was certain he heard:

A pack of witches screeching like maniacs.

The foghorn of a large ocean liner.

Terrible groans, probably someone being tortured.

Sneezes so loud they must be coming from a giant.

He tried to be brave but he wanted to be back at Dee's, where he felt safe. It wasn't quiet in the city, but at least he knew what he was hearing.

He lay quaking on his blanket, which was damp. Horrified, he realized he was so frightened he had drooled all over it.

He crawled over to Maggie and lay down next to her.

"Grawlumph," she muttered in her sleep.

"Maggie," Pretty Boy meowed as softly as his terror permitted.

No answer.

He tried again, a little louder.

Maggie simply stretched and then flopped over. She was exhausted from their journey.

Pretty Boy sighed and curled up at Maggie's feet.

For a long time he kept his eyes wide open and his muscles tensed. The noises didn't go away, but they didn't come closer. He relaxed a little, and then a little more.

He almost dropped off when he heard the ticking. And tocking.

TICK TICK TICK.

TOCK TOCK TOCK.

TICK TOCK.

He thought his head was going to explode.

How long was two weeks, he wondered.

An eternity, that's how long, he answered himself.

What kind of person lived in a place like this, he wondered.

He began counting sheep, to put himself to sleep. That was a mistake. His imaginary sheep first appeared as harmless, friendly creatures drifting across the imaginary fence he built in his mind. But then they changed. Sheep after sheep climbed onto giant bicycles and began riding toward him, aiming right for his tail. He tried to move but couldn't as they came closer and closer, shouting baas that sounded like giant sneezes.

He could tell they hated cats. Specifically, they hated him.

"Pretty Stupid, Pretty Stupid, Pretty Stupid," they chanted over and over.

Those horrible creatures were the last thing Pretty Boy remembered until he heard someone say, "Good morning! You must be Pretty Boy."

He opened one eye and then the other.

Kneeling next to him was a woman with messy hair that was gray and light brown. Her crinkly dark eyes were calm and wise. She pronounced words in a way Pretty Boy had never heard them pronounced before. She seemed old and young at the same time, wrinkled but full of energy.

Without thinking about it, he liked her.

It appeared that his nightmare was over.

"Grandma!" the children cried out as they stumbled out of their bedroom and landed in her arms.

"Did you hear all that hubbub last night?" she asked.

"Nope," said Eli.

"Uh-uh," said Lilly.

"Oh my, you must have been tired," Grandma laughed. "The loons on the lake were nutty, screaming their heads off. And your daddy was snoring like a fiend. Then it got so cold the heat went on, and this old house's pipes objected."

She planted a big kiss on Lilly's cheek.

"And you, my tiny princess, were sneezing so loudly, like an enormous old man!"

"No I wasn't," giggled Lilly. "I mean, no I didn't."

"Absolutely true," said Grandma.

"I told you," Eli said to his sister.

"Do you have a cold, sweetheart?" Grandma asked.

Lilly shook her head.

"I think I'm allergic to the country," she said solemnly. Even her freckles looked somber.

"What's allergic?" teased Eli.

Lilly shook her pigtails in confusion.

"I don't know but that's what I am," she said.

Pretty Boy decided it was time to take a tour of his new surroundings. He walked from the little hallway outside the children's bedroom into a beautiful, sunlit room. The floors were made of wide planks of wood, colored by time. The ceilings were low, making the room feel cozy, but it also felt open, because one entire wall was lined with windows. Through them, he could see down the gently sloping hill to Lost Lake, hidden behind a cluster of soaring evergreen trees.

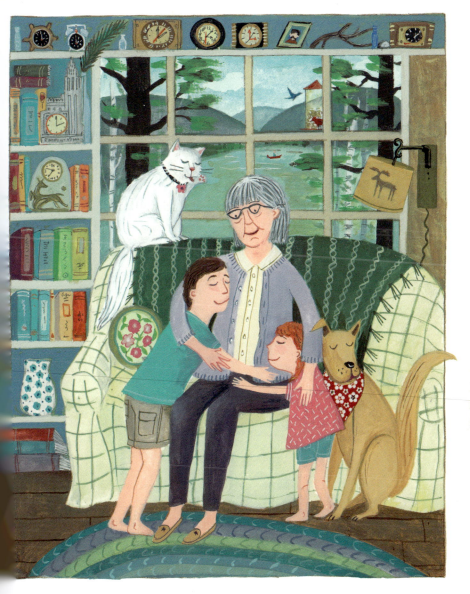

There wasn't much furniture—a big rumpled couch, a couple of comfy chairs, and a long wooden table surrounded by straight-backed chairs. There were, however, many books crammed into floor to ceiling shelves—and almost as many clocks.

"Do you like my little shack?" Grandma asked as Pretty Boy hopped up on the couch and curled up as if he lived there.

"Tell us about the clocks!" Lilly asked.

"Oh no, not again!" said Eli.

"Please!" begged Lilly.

Pretty Boy could see that the children's grandma liked to tell stories, and didn't seem to mind that her grandchildren had heard them before.

She sat next to Pretty Boy and the children joined them.

"Your grandfather was the one who started our collection," she said. Touching Eli's shoulder, she asked, "Do you remember Grandpa?"

"Of course I do," he said. "I helped him build the bird feeder."

Grandma laughed. "You certainly did," she said. "It's quite unique."

Pretty Boy glanced out the window and saw a group of birds perched on the edge of a strange contraption made of wood and metal, rigged to release small amounts of food when the tray was empty.

"I miss Grandpa," Eli said.

"Me, too," said Lilly. Then she sneezed.

"Bless you," said Eli. Then he said, "How could you miss him? You were a baby when he died."

Lilly replied, "That doesn't mean I can't miss him."

She sneezed again.

"That's right," Grandma said as she arched her eyebrows and gave Eli a look that made him stop teasing Lilly.

She returned to her story.

"When we came to the United States from the old country we were very young," she said.

Eli chimed in. "And you didn't have anything."

Grandma ruffled Eli's hair and smiled, though her eyes were sad.

"That's right," she said.

"Well, we had a few things," she corrected herself. "One of them was that clock." She pointed to a small model of the Empire State Building with a clock built into its base.

"One of your grandpa's cousins gave it to him for good luck," she added. "It was a cheap souvenir but to us it was valuable. To us it meant there was a future."

She laughed. "Of course when we saw the Empire State Building for the first time, it reminded us of our little clock and the past."

She fell silent until Lilly asked, "But when did you get the other clocks?"

"I don't remember exactly when your grandfather began collecting clocks, but he had a few rules," Grandma said. "They had to be beautiful, though as you can see, some of them are very ugly."

Pretty Boy stared at a gaudy clock decorated with pink swans and nodded in agreement.

Grandma continued. "He meant beautiful to us," she said. "They had to remind us of a special time."

"And," she added, "they had to cost less than twenty-five dollars. Your grandfather was generous in many ways, but he didn't like to spend money when he didn't have to."

Pretty Boy listened to the ticking and tocking. So *that* was the terrible noise that had haunted him the night before. Now the sounds they made weren't frightening at all. As he looked around the room, he noticed how many clocks there were, all shapes and sizes. He realized how much worse the racket could have been! Luckily, most of the clocks were silent, their hands stopped at different places on the dial.

"Well, children," said Grandma. "How about breakfast, then down to the lake!"

As she got up, she realized something.

"I used to spend a lot of time winding the clocks, but now I don't worry if all of them aren't going," she said. "I don't mind so much anymore when time stands still."

Pretty Boy found himself thinking about Grandma's words, and what they might mean. He began following her around, waiting for further explanation.

Despite his reservations about country life, Pretty Boy enjoyed himself. He was not like Maggie, who became a different dog in Maine. Pretty Boy was astonished the first time they went on a family hike, and he watched his friend become a wild creature. The dog that jumped at loud noises in New York disappeared. Maggie galloped up and down trails and leaped over stone walls without fear. Back at the lake, while Pretty Boy sunned himself on the dock, Maggie dived into the cold water over and over again.

Pretty Boy felt a little jealous.

"Where is my connection to my wild self, the lion within?" he asked himself as he watched Maggie chasing a terrified chipmunk.

He didn't let this concern trouble him too much. It was very relaxing on the dock.

At bedtime, Pretty Boy joined Lilly as she listened to her father or mother read and reread her two favorite books, *Where the Wild Things Are* and *Hey Willy, See the Pyramids*.

If the cat wasn't at her side, Lilly would insist on waiting until he hopped up on the bed next to her. When Lilly heard a favorite passage, she looked at Pretty Boy and asked, "Don't you love that part?"

Almost always, he did. He found that Lilly had excellent taste in literature (and cats).

Pretty Boy's favorite moments, however, came after dinner, when the family gathered on the porch and stared up at the millions of stars that appeared in the vast nothingness above them.

The first evening, after Grandma made up stories about the night sky, she said to Eli, "I hear you have some good music for me to hear. Want to play it while we sit here?"

Eli looked suspiciously at his mother, who shrugged her shoulders.

"You really want to hear it?" he asked his grandma.

"What do you think?" she answered.

Eli told Grandma what had happened when he played the Cello Man's CD at school, not knowing she had already heard the story from his mother.

"They may not have been ready to hear the music," she said to Eli. "You are lucky that you were."

Pretty Boy and Maggie looked at each other.

"Looks like Grandma took over our job," said Maggie.

Pretty Boy yawned.

"Fine by me," he said. "She's a wise woman."

"Eli," said Grandma. "Have you thought about taking lessons?"

The boy didn't respond as he slid the CD into his grandma's computer and turned up the volume.

The cello's voice seemed to reach up to the stars. As Pretty Boy lay on the porch listening, he was both in Maine and in Washington Square, the first place he'd heard the Cello Man play. But he was also locked in the car trunk, not knowing where he was or what might happen to him. He wondered what the music would mean to him next time he heard it.

CHAPTER ELEVEN

Welcome Home

After the Maine vacation was over, Patti and Dee invited Eli's family to join them for a party to celebrate Pretty Boy's return—and to thank them for taking care of him. When Pretty Boy walked in the front door of Pink Patti's, Roxie was waiting for him, wearing a large pink bow around her neck.

"You scared us to death," were Roxie's first words.

"Nice to see you, too," replied Pretty Boy, a touch of sarcasm in his meow.

Roxie walked over and bent her head so it touched his.

Pretty Boy couldn't resist that gesture, so simple but full of love.

"I had a nice vacation but I am happy to be home," he confessed.

At that moment he realized how much he had missed his friends.

Patti knew exactly what would make her guests happy. There was tuna sushi for Pretty Boy, butcher's bones for Roxie and Maggie, Patti's special macaroni and cheese squares for the kids, and platters of roasted vegetables and cheese for the grown-ups. There was pink lemonade for everyone.

Dee asked Patti to make a toast.

"To Pretty Boy and our fine new friends," she said with a big smile.

They ate and drank. Patti and Dee thanked Eli and Lilly and their parents ten thousand times for being such good sports about their uninvited guest.

The grown-ups talked about how funny it was that they all knew George the dog walker but not one another. They said things like, "Isn't the city full of surprises!" Then they complained about rents going up and what a shame it was that nothing was the same as it used to be.

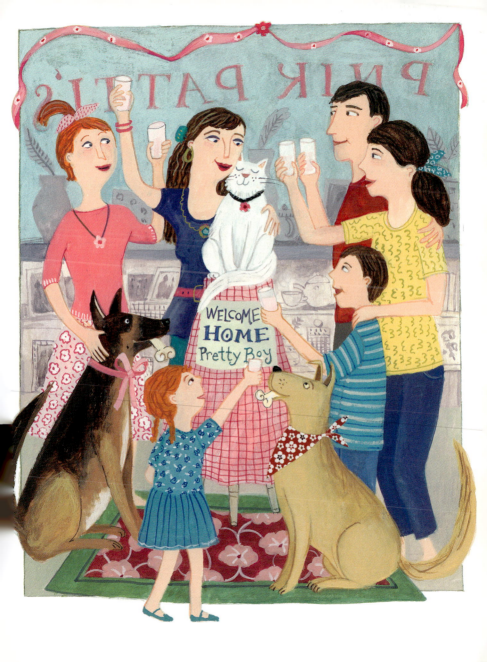

The children grew bored and began roaming around Patti's shop.

"Be careful not to break anything," their mother warned them.

Patti shook her head. "Don't worry," she said. "They'll be fine."

The dogs gnawed contentedly on their bones. Pretty Boy nibbled on sushi, sighing with pleasure.

When the children finished exploring, they rejoined their parents with hopeful looks on their faces.

"Did you find something you want to buy?" their parents asked.

Lilly held out one of Patti's signature cherry blossom notebooks. "I love this," she said.

Her father gave her a squeeze and looked at his son. "What about you?"

Eli blushed, as though the item that had seemed perfect a few minutes earlier had now become embarrassing, juvenile, like a favorite stuffed animal or beloved cap.

"Never mind," he said. "I'll put it back. It's stupid."

Patti overheard the conversation and walked over.

"Funny thing about a lot of stuff in here," she said absentmindedly, as if talking to herself. "It may seem ridiculous but it feels right to me, even if I can't explain why."

Eli lowered his eyes but he was listening. Without saying a word, he held out the object he had hidden behind his back. It was an old-fashioned teacup, decorated with images of musical instruments, mostly violins and cellos.

"You two are amazing," said Patti briskly. "I've been trying to make room for new inventory and have needed to get rid of things that have been here for a long time. You have really helped me out."

Before Lilly or Eli knew what was happening, she'd whisked away the notebook and the teacup and disappeared through a door.

Their father shrugged his shoulders.

Patti returned a few minutes later with two perfectly wrapped boxes. She handed one to Lilly and one to Eli.

"Let me pay you for those," their father said. Patti shook her head in a way that made it clear there was no point in trying.

"Maggie, come here," Patti called out.

Maggie trotted over.

"Sit," Patti commanded, but politely.

Maggie sat.

Patti pulled out a bright pink kerchief from her pocket and tied it around Maggie's neck.

"Roxie wanted me to thank you for taking care of Pretty Boy," she said.

Pretty Boy and Roxie stopped eating to watch.

"No wonder she worries about not making money," Pretty Boy whispered to Roxie. "She's always giving away the merchandise."

Then they were distracted by Dee, carrying a giant platter of cupcakes and a tray of dog treats and catnip.

As everyone plunged into dessert, Pretty Boy and Maggie regaled Roxie with stories about their vacation in Maine.

Pretty Boy spoke with admiration about Maggie's physical feats—the way she swam across the icy lake and fought her way through the dangerous brambles lurking in the woods.

Maggie chimed in with Pretty Boy's exploits—how he overcame his fear of water and took long canoe rides with the children.

"One day," Maggie said dramatically, "Pretty Boy stared down a moose. It was awesome!"

In fact, the family had taken a hike one day with Pretty Boy and Maggie in tow. On the way back to the car they came face-to-face with a giant bull moose. Pretty Boy wasn't paying attention and didn't notice that everyone in the group had stopped except for him. By the time he realized what was going on, he found himself looking straight up into the moose's eyes. Frozen with fear, the cat didn't move. Not one whisker wiggled as he locked eyes with that huge creature with the giant antlers. The moose squinted and pondered. He yawned. Then he turned and walked away.

"Wow," said Roxie. "You might have been eaten."

They all nodded with excitement, though the danger of that had been remote. Moose are vegetarians. It's true they are big and could trample a cat that got in their way. But most likely Pretty Boy would have been in more danger if he'd been a carrot.

There were times when New York could seem cold and lonely, a place where it was easy to get lost in the crowd. This wasn't one of those times. This was the kind of New

York moment where a gathering of friends felt like the center of the universe.

They could have talked all night, but the time came for Maggie and her family to go home. To make the party last a little longer, the group walked together toward Washington Square. A giant moon was hanging low, right above the Arch. The warm night air was peaceful but held a hint of excitement.

Much as Pretty Boy had come to appreciate the country, he realized he felt most alive in the city. He was alert but not fearful, ready for adventure.

He saw the hawk's shadow flit past the moon. Pretty Boy didn't flinch. He shook his head, remembering how scared he'd felt when he had spent the night alone in the park. That seemed so long ago.

As they drew closer to the Arch, his ears widened. He hoped the Cello Man would be there to welcome them back. He caught the faint sound of music floating through the park, growing stronger as they walked. His tail lifted and his paws moved faster. But he soon realized he was listening to a jazz band parked by the statue of General Giuseppe Garibaldi.

Pretty Boy shook off his disappointment and let his paws tap to the beat. His tail swayed in the breeze. He

wondered who General Giuseppe Garibaldi was and why he rated a statue. He turned his face toward the moon.

The blissful hum of the evening was broken by a barrage of barks.

It was Henry, out for a stroll with his owners. They were mild-looking people, not at all what Pretty Boy had imagined. Henry was so excitable! They joined Pretty Boy's group. A few minutes passed while introductions were made and stories exchanged.

The breeze grew insistent, becoming more like a wind.

"I hear there's going to be a big storm," one of Henry's owners said.

"That's what they always say," laughed Dee. "And then there's a sprinkle."

"Or the other way around," said Patti, a note of worry in her voice.

Lilly sneezed and yawned, but when her mother said it was time to go, the little girl cried out, "No! I want this night to go on forever."

Pretty Boy agreed.

The adults laughed and said good night.

Roxie and Pretty Boy followed Patti and Dee toward home on a wide cement path lit by the old-fashioned electric lamps. Cat and dog made a pretty picture, with the light bouncing off their well-brushed fur, which rippled in the wind. The concrete felt solid beneath Pretty Boy's paws. He couldn't imagine wanting to be anywhere else.

CHAPTER TWELVE

After the Storm

By morning, the breeze that became a wind had blown up into a wild, raging storm. Dee didn't bother to open the shop that day. Pretty Boy knew it was bad when Dee invited him up into her apartment, right above the store. This was a rare event. She liked to keep their boundaries clear. But she couldn't bear to think of the poor cat alone as the windows rattled and the sky roared.

They didn't dare venture outside. Dee caught up on bills and did some reading. Pretty Boy stayed calm because Dee did, despite the nerve-racking cracks of lightning and the violent blasts of thunder.

As the day wore on, Pretty Boy saw Dee was more nervous than she let on. Every hour or so, she checked on the weather report, which remained ominous.

Then the electricity went out.

"That's it, kid," Dee said with a tense laugh. "It's you and me and Mother Nature."

Pretty Boy had never seen Dee get scared, but he would bet his whiskers that she was scared now. He certainly was.

The storm went on all day and was still raging when Dee announced that she was tired.

"Good night, Pretty Boy," she said, closing the door to her bedroom.

The instant she left him alone, Pretty Boy was sure the storm became wilder.

The next thunder clap sent him leaping to his feet. He skittered across the apartment, landing outside the door to Dee's room.

He paused.

"Can I go in there?" he asked himself. "I don't want Dee to think . . ."

Pow!

Now Pretty Boy knew what people meant when they said, "The heavens shook!"

He began scratching at the door, unable to control himself.

It didn't take long for Dee to open the door a crack and wave him inside. With as much dignity as he could fake, Pretty Boy scampered over to a colorful throw rug next to the bed. He curled up there while Dee climbed back under the covers.

The next roar of thunder was even louder than the ones that had come before. This time Pretty Boy jumped straight up into the air, landing by Dee's feet.

He lay there shivering in terror, hoping she wouldn't toss him onto the floor.

Her toes stroked his fur. Without saying a word, they had let each other know how much they had come to depend on one another.

Right before dawn, Pretty Boy was yanked out of a deep slumber by an explosive noise. The building shook so hard it seemed ready to splinter into pieces.

Then it was over, like that. The raging storm dissolved into a steady rain.

Pretty Boy fell back asleep but was wakened again by a sound that disturbed him more than anything that had come before.

Dee was sobbing.

Dee—the woman who never let anything get to her, who always reassured everyone else—was falling apart because of a storm.

Pretty Boy lay completely still, not sure of what he should do. He was upset that Dee was unhappy but didn't know how to make her feel better.

I shall never understand human nature, he thought to himself, *no matter how long I live.*

The next morning he got a clearer picture of what had upset Dee so much. She had realized right away what the explosive, splintering sound was. It was the shattering of glass.

While Pretty Boy had been sleeping, Dee had made her way downstairs and turned on the lights, which had blown out and then come on again. She gasped when she saw the destruction. In the waning moments of the storm, the wind had grabbed hold of a street sign and flung it right through the big window of Dee's hair salon. She stared at the broken glass and puddles of water strewn around her shop. The damage didn't upset

her as much as her reaction to it. For the first time in her life she didn't feel like picking up the pieces.

"I'm tired," she said, though no one was listening.

Unable to deal with the mess just then, she went back to bed and cried herself to sleep.

The calm of the next morning was broken by the noise of a ringing buzzer. Patti and Roxie were outside.

Dee buzzed them in. Without a word, Patti hugged her friend. The two women huddled together and talked to each other in low voices. Pretty Boy couldn't make out what they were saying, except that Pink Patti's hadn't been damaged.

"We're going for a walk to Washington Square," said Patti. "I figure there won't be much business today. Want to join us?"

Dee shook her head.

"I'm going to try and clean up and see about getting the window fixed," she said.

She looked at Pretty Boy, who was already standing by the front door.

"But I see someone who wants to go."

She smiled, but Pretty Boy saw this was a reflex. There was no joy in her voice.

Pretty Boy wanted to help Dee, but he was tired of being cooped up.

"She needs some time alone," he reassured himself as he joined Roxie and Patti.

As they walked to the park, Patti kept sighing and shaking her head. The streets were full of stuff, as if the storm had lifted up trash cans and trees and smacked them down again.

"Poor old New York," Patti murmured. "Poor us."

Pretty Boy didn't understand what she was feeling until they reached the park. It was too quiet. The usual chorus of morning birdsong was absent. Not a peep.

The calm felt ominous.

Sunshine cast a bright light on the wreckage. The storm had been vicious. Plants were scattered everywhere, pulled up by their roots. Handsome old trees stood sadly, limbs cracked and dangling. The paths were littered with branches and garbage blown out of trash cans. The bronze face of General Garibaldi was hidden behind a broken bough.

Squirrels wandered aimlessly, looking confused. Pigeons crept around without uttering a sound, not one measly *coo*.

Even the rats looked pitiful.

Pretty Boy looked up at the roof of Bobst. He saw the hawk standing there.

Pretty Boy didn't gloat at his enemy's forlorn appearance. He wondered if the hawk's nest had blown down.

At that moment, the world seemed too fragile to bear. Pretty Boy was so distraught by all the damage even his paws ached.

Then he heard voices.

Patti had joined a group of people helping the park rangers drag debris onto a pile. Roxie didn't hesitate either. She grabbed branches with her teeth and

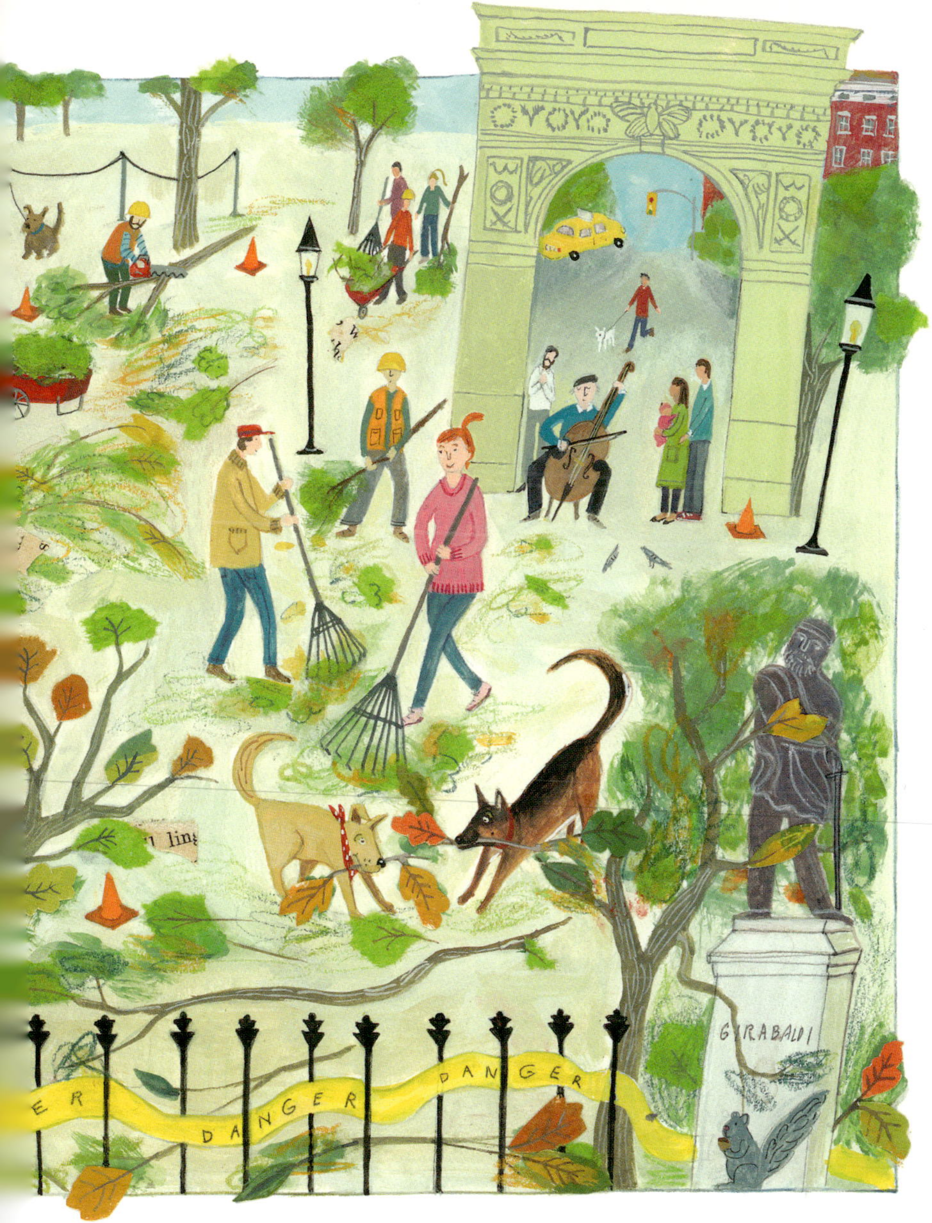
ling
GIRABALDI
ER
DANGER
DANGER

brought them to Patti. But when Patti tried to take them from Roxie's mouth and drop them on the pile, the dog galloped away, the sticks clamped in her mouth.

The people watching began to laugh. Without meaning to, Roxie had helped in her own way, cheering them up by doing what she always did when she found a piece of wood in her mouth.

Pretty Boy shook his head. Dogs and their sticks! He began sweeping twigs and leaves with his tail.

The work was slow going, but they kept at it. Pretty Boy's fur became matted with dirt, but he didn't care. Physical exertion pushed aside both his sadness and his vanity. Hard as it was, he found he enjoyed the labor, no matter that his pile remained the smallest one of the lot, regardless of how hard he swept. (It didn't help that he couldn't resist the urge to pause once in a while to bat some pebbles across the path.)

He was so absorbed in his task, he didn't notice the music at first. He didn't know how long he had been listening when he realized the Cello Man had taken his regular spot under the Arch.

The air filled with the Bach cello suites. It didn't take long for Pretty Boy to realize the music was expressing all the emotions that he had been experiencing that day: mournfulness, hope, despair, and excitement. Yes, excitement! Pretty Boy felt that in his small way, with his large tail, he was fighting back.

Volunteer workers came and went all day, but the Cello Man never budged. The hours passed, but he seemed tireless.

Pretty Boy stayed, too, even after Patti and Roxie urged him to come home with them.

When he couldn't sweep anymore, the cat positioned himself next to the Cello Man, who gave him a warm greeting.

Pretty Boy was pleased to see that his tail hadn't forgotten how to keep time. Soon, the musician gave the cat a nod each time he was about to begin a new piece, and then waited for Pretty Boy's tail to set the tempo.

The afternoon passed by quickly. A truck came to cart off the piles that Pretty Boy and the others had built from the mess the storm had left in its wake. The park still looked bruised and battered, but less pathetic than it had a few hours earlier.

People came and went, pausing under the Arch to listen to the Cello Man's music, and then moving on. Finally a moment arrived when the cat and musician were sitting alone.

The Cello Man hadn't said much all day, apart from thanking people who bought a CD or answering a question about the music. He had been playing almost nonstop, with a determination that went beyond the pleasure of making music.

He wasn't the type to explain himself, but he found himself talking to Pretty Boy about why he felt the need to be in the park after the storm.

"When I was young I had to go to war," he said. "I arrived and was handed a gun that had blood on it."

He paused, as though he had gone somewhere far away.

"It was a disaster," he said. "The generals knew there was going to be a major offensive, but we weren't prepared. I can't describe what it was like. We froze. We were terrified. We shot our weapons like blind men. I must have killed someone but I don't know. I don't want to know."

Pretty Boy listened patiently, looking into the Cello Man's eyes, which were dark with sorrow.

"Then I got lucky," he said. "There was an explosion and for me, the war was over. I woke up in a hospital on clean white sheets. I took a shower for the first time in months and dreaded getting better. I never wanted to hold a gun again."

The faraway expression on his face disappeared. Looking at Pretty Boy, he laughed again, this time with warmth.

"Oh, boy," he said. "I am getting old. I'm talking to a cat!"

Pretty Boy meowed and rubbed his head against the Cello Man's leg.

The musician smiled and scratched Pretty Boy behind the ears.

"I was remembering the doctor I met in the hospital," he said. "He was a musician, too. When he heard I played the cello he managed to get one for me to play. When he heard me, he got me assigned to a quartet that played for the troops. . . . I always say, music saved my life."

His voice trailed off. They sat in silence for a minute or two. Then he picked up the cello.

"Maestro," he said to Pretty Boy, "give me the beat."

When Eli and his family arrived in Washington Square, Maggie was the first to see Pretty Boy. The cat nodded but didn't stop his tail from keeping time, not even when Lilly kept waving at him and blowing him kisses.

The Cello Man's face lit up when he saw them. He tilted his head in their direction, but didn't miss a note.

When he finished the piece, he asked where they'd been. When Eli's dad told him, he said, "I love Maine. My quartet used to play there."

Pretty Boy perked up at this. Before today, it hadn't really occurred to him that the Cello Man had a life outside Washington Square. Now the cat understood there was so much he didn't know.

The Cello Man turned to Eli. "Have you thought more about taking lessons?"

The boy shrugged and looked down at the ground.

Pretty Boy decided to take action. He walked over to the cello and began stroking the strings with his tail. Barely a whisper emerged from the cello, but all the people burst out laughing.

The Cello Man winked at Eli and held out his bow.

"Want to see if you can do better than the cat?" he asked with a grin.

Eli walked over and placed his fingers on the smooth wooden neck.

The Cello Man guided his hand onto the strings.

The sound that emerged wasn't much, but the boy looked as pleased as if he'd produced a virtuoso performance.

"Could you teach me to play?" Eli asked.

The Cello Man looked surprised. He stared at Eli, making silent calculations.

"How old are you?" he asked.

Eli told him.

"Well," the Cello Man replied, "I'm almost eighty. I don't know how much arithmetic you know, but by my counting that makes more than seventy years between us," he said lightly. "It could be a little risky."

Eli didn't respond because he didn't know what the musician was talking about. How dangerous could playing the cello be?

"Let me think about it," the Cello Man said.

The expression on his face was hard to decipher. He looked at Eli's parents. "Take him to the music school on Barrow Street," he said.

Then he turned to Eli.

"Believe me," he said. "This is for the best."

CHAPTER THIRTEEN

Moving On

"N o!" Pretty Boy cried out.

"It can't be true," Maggie said.

They had been dreading this day for so long they'd forgotten to think about it anymore. All that worry was wasted because the news shocked them anyway.

Roxie and Patti were leaving New York.

Pretty Boy was heartbroken.

"Why?" he asked, though he knew the answer.

The three friends were standing in one corner of the dog park, which was almost deserted. A strong wind was blowing; autumn had arrived. Henry hadn't come out that day.

Roxie explained what had happened.

"When we came home from the park after the storm, Patti said to me, 'Doggie dear, I don't want to wear out my welcome.'"

The big wise dog seemed small and uncertain.

"I don't get it," said Maggie.

"The landlord has been coming around a lot," Roxie said. "It's been hard to pay the rent. I think she's tired of struggling."

Maggie made a despairing sound.

"Isn't there anything we can do?" she asked.

Roxie touched Maggie's nose with hers.

"We're dogs, Maggie," she said, recovering her poise. "We are subject to the whims of fate and decisions of humans."

George walked over and knelt down next to them.

"If I didn't know better," he said, "I'd think you knew what's about to happen. You look so sad."

George realized that urgent times required exceptional action. So he reached into his pocket and pulled out a handful of dog (and cat) biscuits. The animals couldn't help themselves. They jumped at the unexpected treats. Despite their distress, they enjoyed every bite.

It all happened so fast that Pretty Boy didn't know what to think. Later, there would come a time when he would feel happy to remember Roxie and Patti and the gifts they gave him. Someday he would be able to reminisce about how they convinced Dee to give him shelter, and how Dee set aside her reservations about owning a pet, because she couldn't help herself.

But he wasn't in the future yet. He was in the now, and it hurt.

Events had been moving quickly. The details jumbled together in his mind. But he came to regard the hurricane as a dividing line between one way of life and another.

This is how he remembered the chain of events:

After the storm, Dee's salon window had remained boarded up for several days. So many windows had blown out during the storm she had to wait in line until hers could be replaced.

Dee was a practical person, who didn't believe much in signs and portents. But she couldn't shake the feeling that someone was telling her something. One day she woke up, stood in front of her damaged shop, and made a decision.

"I am leaving New York," she said to herself.

Her decision was confirmed when she told Patti what she was thinking.

Without hesitation, Patti said, "I've also been feeling it's time to move on."

The two friends cried and hugged one another, knowing the decision they had made at the same time meant they would go their separate ways.

They were shocked but not surprised. For months—maybe even a couple of years—the two of them had been talking a lot about wanting a change of pace, finding a place that moved slower and cost less. They discussed how they loved New York and always would, but maybe they were ready to live somewhere else.

Strange how in an instant speculation became reality, idle conversation became a plan.

They didn't consult with Pretty Boy, but they didn't forget about him. He discovered the upheaval the day he was about to be taken to his new home.

"You're very popular," Dee told him, when she explained what was going on. "Half my customers wanted to take you."

"But none of them seemed right," added Patti, who had dropped by to give moral support.

Dee knelt down and rubbed Pretty Boy behind the ears. "I would take you if I could," she said, sadly, without explaining why she couldn't.

Pretty Boy's fur stood straight up. He walked away from Dee and glared at Patti.

"Betrayers!" he hissed.

The cat turned to Roxie, who had been sitting quietly.

"What do you know?" he demanded.

Roxie had a peculiar look on her face, half grin, half frown.

"I think you'll like it," she said, then corrected herself. "I think you'll like them."

Before Pretty Boy could reply, there was a knock at the hair salon door.

It was Lilly and her mom, who was holding a large container of some kind. Pretty Boy had never seen a cat carrying case before. Maggie was with them, her tail wagging with excitement.

They looked nervous. Lilly hung back, half hiding behind her mother.

"Lilly is so excited," her mother said.

Then she corrected herself. "We're all very excited."

Pretty Boy looked puzzled.

Roxie explained. "Maggie's family has offered to take you in," she said. "When Lilly found out they were looking for a home for you, she went on a campaign. She wouldn't take no for an answer."

Pretty Boy looked at Maggie.

"I just found out this morning," Maggie said. "Honest!" Then she added. "I have always wanted a brother."

Pretty Boy was having a hard time taking it all in. His chest swelled with pride when he heard what a fine impression he'd made on Lilly, even as his eyes filled with tears at the prospect of saying good-bye to his friends. He couldn't imagine life without them.

"I guess it's time, old boy," Patti said, kneeling down, her cheeks damp from tears.

There were hugs and tears and promises of future visits.

Then Lilly's mother opened the door to the case and motioned for Pretty Boy to go inside.

He cocked his head and didn't budge.

Dee laughed.

"I don't think he knows what it is," she explained. "He comes and goes as he pleases."

Lilly's mother looked surprised.

"No leash? No crate?" she asked.

Patti and Dee shook their heads.

There was an awkward silence.

Lilly broke it.

"Don't worry, Mom," she said. "I'll walk next to Pretty Boy and make sure he doesn't run away."

Her mother was torn between her natural inclination to be careful and her desire to make Pretty Boy's move as easy as possible. The decision to take him in hadn't been an easy one. They already had a busy, crowded household. Lilly, however, had made the case for Pretty Boy with force and logic. But three simple words clinched the deal.

"I need him," she told her parents.

Now Lilly's mother looked at her and looked at Pretty Boy. She snapped the door of the cat carrier shut.

"Okay," she said. "I give in."

She wagged her finger at Pretty Boy. "But if you do one thing that scares me, in you go, okay?"

Pretty Boy didn't answer. He was preoccupied with his good-byes. He walked over to Patti and then Dee, rubbing his head against their legs one final time.

To Roxie he said, "I'll never forget you."

She sniffed and lifted her head. "As if you could," she said.

And then she said, "The same goes for me."

Lilly's mother said, "I guess it's time for us to leave."

"Wait!" Patti said. "I forgot. I have something for you."

She went to the back of the shop and returned with something in her hand. She knelt so she could slip off

Pretty Boy's velvet collar. Then she replaced the cherry blossom tag with a new one that was exactly the same except for the telephone number.

"George gave me your number," Patti explained to Lilly's mother, who leaned over to kiss her on the cheek.

"Can we go?" Lilly asked, tugging on her mother's arm impatiently.

With that, Pretty Boy set out for his new home.

CHAPTER FOURTEEN

One of the Family

There was a period of adjustment. It was one thing for them to all live together on vacation in Maine. Things were different now. Pretty Boy had to get used to a complicated series of schedules and expectations. The parents had to be here at a certain time, and the children had to be there. Animals were expected to conform to the rules.

Hardest for Pretty Boy was the lack of privacy. At Dee's—except for the night of the storm—Pretty Boy and Dee went their separate ways after dark. Pretty Boy had the run of the shop when Dee went to bed in her own apartment. If the cat decided to go for an all-night prowl, no one asked questions.

Pretty Boy would never forget the first—and last—time he slipped out the window and stayed out one night. The household adults had a fit.

"Where were you?" they exclaimed. "We thought you were dead!"

Lilly cried.

Pretty Boy felt awful. He looked at them in a way he hoped would assure them he wouldn't do it again. Yet he felt his tail droop a notch.

They were kind people and he liked their company, but sometimes he needed a break. When he complained to Maggie one day, she looked at him blankly.

"I clearly remember you objecting to exactly this kind of thing," Pretty Boy said to her.

"I don't know what you are talking about," she said huffily.

Together in close quarters, Pretty Boy realized that Maggie was a mixed bag in the memory department. When Eli's father re-entered their house five minutes after he left because he forgot his gloves, she leaped on him with such joy you'd think he'd been gone for months. In that way she seemed to suffer from perma-

nent amnesia—a condition apparently shared by the humans she loved, because they always accepted her kisses with the joy of fresh infatuation.

On the other hand, Maggie had a powerful ability to remember a slight. Despite her good nature, she was a first-class grudge collector. For example, there was the small black-and-white dog that bit her on the ear when Maggie was a pup and they were the same size. Pretty Boy had witnessed Maggie's refusal to enter the dog park if that little mutt was there, even though she was now triple his height and weight.

Pretty Boy accepted these personality quirks and minor restrictions as the price he had to pay for the unexpected pleasure he found in being part of a family. In the same way Maggie curled up with Eli every night, Pretty Boy found his place with Lilly. He became accustomed to falling asleep to the sound of her sneezing and snoring, and the way she talked through her dreams. He was pleased to discover that when she had nightmares, she turned to him. He enjoyed the dramas, large and small, the fights and reconciliations, the sweet gestures that made their little household feel like a fortress against the uncertainty out there.

CHAPTER FIFTEEN

Cello Lessons

What is the matter with you?" Maggie asked Pretty Boy, who hadn't stopped meowing since they left the house.

It was Eli's first day of cello lessons. He'd asked his mother if Pretty Boy and Maggie could come with them. Pretty Boy was as nervous as the boy, maybe a little bit more.

They arrived early.

The music school looked as if it hadn't changed in a hundred years. It was located in a redbrick town house on a charming street, filled with flowering trees.

The small lobby on the main floor was decorated with photographs taken throughout the decades of children holding instruments. Hairstyles and fashion changed, but the instruments remained the same.

Pretty Boy loved it the instant he walked in the door. He had a soft spot for old-fashioned things. But they were there only a minute or two when the receptionist cleared her throat and said, "Excuse me."

She was a brisk woman with short gray hair.

"Sorry," she said. "No animals allowed in the building."

Pretty Boy sidled up to her and meowed his most charming meow.

The receptionist didn't look as stern when she cracked a smile.

"We have a little garden out back," she said, pointing toward a narrow corridor leading to a door. "The dog and cat can wait out there."

"Thank you," said Eli's mom.

Maggie and Pretty Boy followed her down the corridor and then stopped when they noticed Eli wasn't coming with them.

"Are you coming?" Eli's mom asked him.

"No," he said. "I'd rather wait inside by myself."

"Wait a second," Pretty Boy said to Maggie. "Isn't *he* the one who insisted we come with him?"

"He's just nervous," Maggie said. "He's probably wondering what his teacher will be like, what if he makes a fool out of himself."

Pretty Boy nodded. Then he heard a shy voice emerging from a big chair across the lobby.

"Hey there," it said. "Don't you recognize me?"

Pretty Boy saw Eli staring at a girl with dark hair.

"Oh yeah," he said. "Hi."

Her name was Olivia. She had been in his class at school.

"What are you here for?"

She was very formal.

"Cello," he mumbled.

She smiled.

"I remember when you brought that music into class last year," she said. "I liked it very much."

"You *did*?" Eli said. Silently, he thought, *Why didn't you tell me then!*

As if she'd heard what he was thinking, she said, "I was too shy to say anything."

Eli nodded.

"What are you taking?" he asked.

"Piano lessons," she said, shaking her head. "My mother is making me."

The receptionist interrupted.

"Ma'am," she said, "are you taking the animals outside?"

Pretty Boy, Maggie, and Eli's mom were still standing in the corridor, eavesdropping on Eli's conversation.

Then the receptionist said, "Eli, you can go up to the second floor. Sam is waiting in room thirty-four."

He didn't budge.

"Don't worry," the receptionist smiled. "He's a wonderful teacher."

Eli picked up the case that held the cello his parents had rented. The Cello Man had been right. They did make small cellos.

Thinking about the Cello Man made Eli feel hurt all over again. Why couldn't he have taught him? So what if he was old?

The boy gave a small wave to Olivia as he walked to the staircase.

"Good luck," she said.

When he reached upstairs he stood for a couple of minutes in front of the dark wooden door marked 34. He took a deep breath before knocking.

"Come in," said a voice that sounded familiar.

Eli walked inside and rubbed his eyes, not sure he was seeing correctly.

"Hello, Eli," said the Cello Man with a welcoming smile. "Nice to see you again."

Eli didn't say anything, he was so surprised.

"Cat got your tongue?" Sam teased. "Where is that cat of yours, by the way?"

Eli ignored the question.

"*You're* Sam?" he finally managed to ask.

"Didn't you think I had a name," Sam asked him.

Yes! said Eli to himself. *The Cello Man.*

Out loud, he simply mumbled, "Well, yes, but . . ."

Then he said, "I thought you said you were too old to teach me."

"Is that what I said?" Sam asked, a note of amusement in his voice. "I don't think so. I think what I said was, 'Let me think about it.'"

Eli didn't know what else to say. So he just stood there.

"What are you waiting for?" Sam asked. "We have a lot of work to do and there isn't much time."

He only meant that the room was booked the following hour, but Eli unpacked his cello with a sense of urgency. He gripped the arm of his instrument as though he had been appointed to carry out a vital mission.

Sam pressed his lips together, holding back a smile.

"Take it easy, Eli," he said. "Let's start at the beginning."

Eli began to laugh.

"What's so funny?" Sam asked.

Eli pointed toward the window. Pretty Boy had scampered up one of the dogwood trees that flowered in the music school's backyard. The cat was sitting on one of the branches, waiting for the music to begin.

Pretty Boy looked forward to Saturday mornings and the cello lessons. Every week he and Maggie would wait in the yard, while Eli climbed the stairs to his lesson. Maggie curled up and took a nap while Pretty Boy took his place up on the dogwood tree. As he watched and listened, the mysterious rhythms of life began to fall into place.

For the first time, Pretty Boy truly felt he was more than an accessory. He had a definite purpose. Maggie had made it clear that Eli's room was her territory at night, while Pretty Boy kept Lilly company. But Maggie wasn't that interested in Eli's music. So when the boy daydreamed instead of practicing, Pretty Boy nudged him with his head until Eli had no choice but to pick his bow up again. When Eli lost count, Pretty Boy sat next to him, moving his tail in perfect time.

Pretty Boy's job was not easy. The sounds Eli made at first were nothing like the Cello Man's. Every time he picked up his bow, Maggie ran out of the room. But the boy learned quickly. He soon was able to read notes and to find his way on the cello strings. His fingers began to curve the way Sam wanted. Squawks and squeaks began to sound like music.

The better Eli played, the more demanding Sam became.

Pretty Boy was taken aback when he saw how fierce the gentle Cello Man could become when he felt his student hadn't paid attention. As the weeks and months passed, Room 34 alternated between battleground, lecture hall, cathedral, theater, torture chamber.

He thought Sam would go through the roof when Eli showed up at his lesson with the thumb on his bowing arm wrapped in a bandage.

Without an ounce of pity, Sam asked what had happened.

Eli explained he'd hurt himself during soccer practice. He wore a sheepish grin as he looked at his teacher, as if expecting sympathy or praise for coming to lesson with an injury.

Sam looked grim but said nothing except, "Start with a scale."

The boy began by playing the G major scale. He played perfectly on the way up but forgot to make the F a sharp on the way down.

Pretty Boy saw Sam suppress a smile.

"You owe me an F sharp," he said, sternly.

Eli responded with a somber stare.

"And don't be so stingy with the bow," Sam added.

The boy tried a second time.

This time, Sam nodded his approval.

"Very good," he said, "Very good. But now what you have to do is make it what we call *legato,* smooth."

Sam demonstrated.

"Got it?" he asked. "Good. Otherwise, it's fine. Except for your arm. Try not to raise your right arm so high. Oh yes, something else. I keep my fingers down more than you do."

Eli tried again.

"You have a nice sound," said Sam. "But you don't do anything with it."

Eli's eyes looked ready to cry. Pretty Boy wanted to say, "Lighten up, Sam!" But he didn't.

Then the teacher asked Eli, "Any questions?"

Eli was unable to think of a single one.

Sam shook his head. "If you don't ask questions, you'll never learn anything."

But a few minutes later, when Eli asked a question, Sam scolded him.

"I explained that to you already," he said. "Don't you listen?"

Pretty Boy watched as Sam piled on the instructions. *Lift your fingers, have them make contact. Play smooth as running water; use your bow like a paintbrush; think of music as sentences that need commas and periods. There's no air between the notes, that's where the music is.*"

The cat was impressed with the old man's use of metaphor, but he felt sorry for the kid, who often looked overwhelmed. Eli was game, though. No matter how much Sam criticized and suggested, praised and retracted, Eli didn't waver; he picked up his bow and took another crack at it. Sometimes, when the lesson was over, Pretty Boy couldn't tell who was more exhausted, teacher or student.

Fall became winter. On very cold days, Sam would wink at Eli and open the window to let Pretty Boy inside the music room. "Don't tell them downstairs," the old man would say.

Pretty Boy watched and learned along with Eli.

Some days the lessons were so rough Eli would leave the room pale and shaken, feeling like a failure. Pretty Boy wanted to tell Sam to lay off, though he didn't know how to make him understand.

But he came to realize the teacher usually seemed to know when he had pushed too hard.

One day, after a particularly grueling session, Pretty Boy heard a change in the tone of Sam's voice. He saw that the old man's face had softened.

"Before I went to the war, I had the chance to take lessons from one of the best cellists who ever lived," he said. "His name was Emanuel Feuermann. I was already a grown man, but Feuermann was so tough he made me cry. He made me feel like I didn't know anything. But I learned more from those seven lessons than from all the other teachers I had."

It was hard to read the expression on Eli's face, but he nodded.

CHAPTER SIXTEEN

Song of the Wind

Pretty Boy was impressed by the boy's resilience. But he soon realized Eli's motivation wasn't purely musical. Every week he insisted on arriving early, hoping for a chance to "accidentally" bump into Olivia. They discovered they had similar complaints about their teachers, praise for their pets, annoyances with their younger sibling—and a mutual delight in spending time with each other, though that was something they never discussed.

One day Olivia asked Eli if he would like to play a duet with her at the next recital.

"Yes," he said immediately. "That sounds like a great idea."

They had both learned a piece called "Song of the Wind" and agreed that was what they should play.

By the time Eli got home that day he was a nervous wreck.

"What's bothering you?" his mother asked.

Eli blushed and mumbled and rubbed his eyes. Finally he spit it out.

"This girl who used to be in my class wants to play a duet in the next recital with me," he said.

His mother smiled. "That sounds like a great idea," she said.

Eli startled her by yelling, "No it isn't! It is a terrible idea. Don't you remember what happened when I took the Cello Man—Sam's—music to school and everyone laughed at me and called me an idiot?"

"Well, that's not exactly what . . ." his mother began. Eli interrupted.

"Yes it is," he yelled. "Maybe they didn't say those exact words but it's what they were thinking."

"Is that what Olivia was thinking?" his mother asked.

Eli went to his room and shut the door.

"You don't get it!" he muttered.

During this outburst, Maggie and Pretty Boy lay on the couch, pretending to sleep. After Eli left the room, they tried to figure out a plan to make Eli feel better.

It turned out they didn't have to do anything. Not long after Eli's outburst, he began to practice his cello.

The dog, the cat, and Eli's mother sat on the couch listening and wondering: Would "Song of the Wind" ever sound less like a howling wind and more like a song?

CHAPTER SEVENTEEN

Pretty Boy Saves the Day

I t had been a long winter. But then, winters always seem to drag on forever while summers fly by. The days stretched out a bit more every day; the chill in the air diminished. The city seemed revived and refreshed, as though waking from a prolonged nap.

For Eli, however, the warm weather was cause for alarm because it meant the recital was approaching. Pretty Boy couldn't tell who was more nervous—him or Eli or Sam.

The day before Eli was supposed to rehearse with Olivia, Sam was on the warpath.

"What bothers me is that some notes are too fast, some too slow," Sam said. "What am I doing here? You haven't practiced enough. When I tell you to do something, I mean, Do it! Think of me as king!"

Lips trembling, Eli played a section of the piece, a part he thought he knew well.

"Don't be lazy," Sam said. "Better too loud than too soft. What you're doing has no meaning. You're just playing the notes. More feeling. Breathe."

Then, he said, "There's no air between the notes, that's where the music is."

Eli absently drew his bow back and forth on the cello strings, making squeaky little sounds that caused Pretty Boy's fur to stand on end.

Sam snapped. "Sit forward in your chair," he ordered. "If you are so relaxed you have no control."

"I'm not sure you're ready for the recital," Sam said as Eli was walking out the door.

"Good-bye to you, too," Eli muttered.

Sam didn't hear him but Pretty Boy did. He began to meow plaintively.

Sam sank onto the piano bench next to the cat.

"Eli has an ear but he doesn't use it," he said, stroking Pretty Boy's head.

Pretty Boy cocked his head.

Sam gave him a rueful smile. "I know you think I was too hard on him. He's doing very well, but there's no easy way to learn. You have to love it. Maybe love too much."

Pretty Boy couldn't help himself. He'd had a huge breakfast and now he had to digest this emotional overload. He opened his mouth and out came a huge belch.

Sam looked surprised and then burst out laughing.

"I know how you feel," he said.

Light poured through the tall, narrow window. Sam opened it enough so that Pretty Boy could slip out. The old man sat on a folding chair and began to play scales on his cello. His fingers were slender but strong, despite the arthritis he complained about regularly.

"Not bad for an old man," he said to himself.

Pretty Boy sat on the sill for a few minutes, watching and listening. Then he hopped onto a tree branch and went on his way, satisfied that the old man knew what he was doing. He didn't know if this was a hope or a prediction, but he felt calm.

Pretty Boy noticed that Eli behaved strangely before rehearsals with Olivia. Sometimes the boy changed his shirt two or three times before they got together to practice. When she bumped into Eli outside the music school, his face would turn bright red. Yet Pretty Boy observed that once Olivia came into the picture, Eli never objected to practicing.

The morning of the recital, Eli sneaked Pretty Boy inside the building for a peek at the recital hall, which seemed very grand to both boy and cat. In back of the stage, long blue velvet curtains, slightly faded, swooped down from high ceilings, framing large windows that looked out onto the garden. Portraits of present and former teachers adorned the walls, including one of Sam—a much younger version of himself—with dark hair and a far-off look in his eyes.

The wood floors gleamed, showing the results of a fresh sanding and polish. Eli sighed and went to sit in the small room next to the stage, where the musicians waited their turn to play. Olivia was already there.

She whispered, "I'm a little nervous, are you?"

Eli lied. "No," he said. "Don't worry. We'll be fine."

She smiled and nodded.

Eli walked over to the window and opened it enough for Pretty Boy to scoot outside. The cat jumped onto a tree branch. It was the same tree where he perched for Eli's lessons, just a lower branch, a floor below the room where Sam gave lessons. From this branch, Pretty Boy had a perfect seat to watch the recital, even though he would be looking at the musicians' backs.

The cat saw that almost every chair in the hall was occupied. On the ground below him sat Maggie and a couple of other dogs whose owners were on the roster of young musicians playing that morning.

Maggie jumped up a few times, trying to see inside, her futile gestures accompanied by whimpers and barks of frustration. The window was much too high.

Pretty Boy shook his head, always amazed at the inability of dogs to calculate distance. For him, leaping onto narrow ledges and other daredevil acts barely took thought, the way some people can do the *New York Times* Sunday crossword without breaking into a sweat.

"Shhhh," he hissed. "It's about to begin."

Maggie collapsed on the ground, a heap of self-pity.

Pretty Boy was struck with remorse, remembering all of Maggie's kindness to him. "Hey," he whispered. "Let me tell you what's going on."

Here's what he reported:

"The place is packed," he said. "Mostly parents, or that's who I think they are because they are hold-ing video cam-eras. Quite a few older folks, maybe grandparents, lots of little kids—probably brothers and sisters—squirm-ing in their seats. I see some of the teachers in the front row."

"Is Sam there?" Maggie asked.

"I'm not sure," Pretty Boy said. "He's not with the other teachers."

His eyes swept up and down the room before he saw him.

"Sam's here," he said. "Way in the back."

Then he remembered. "Oh

yeah. He told Eli that's where he likes to sit because he doesn't want to be a distraction."

Pretty Boy added, "I think he sits there because he gets so worried."

The recital began.

Eli and Olivia were fifth on the list, after a string of pianists. Pretty Boy enjoyed the formal gestures that lent a sense of grandeur to the school's performances for family and friends.

The director gravely announced each performer and his or her piece, equal respect granted the six-year-old gamely attacking "Twinkle, Twinkle, Little Star," a nine-year-old playing "Für Elise," and the twelve-year-old showman banging out "Toccata for piano" by Khachaturian. The stool set up by the Steinway grand piano was ceremoniously raised and lowered according to the requirements of each performer.

Then it was Eli and Olivia's turn. Pretty Boy thought they looked charming as they walked out together, both wearing black slacks and pressed white shirts. She was tall and slender, with her dark hair done in simple braids. He clutched his small cello with one hand and tried to pat down a resistant cowlick with the other.

They bowed awkwardly and then took their places.

Eli pulled out his end pin, the metal rod that was supposed to anchor the cello to the floor. Olivia held her hands above the keys, waiting for Eli's nod, as they'd practiced so many times. Eli soberly placed his hands on the cello, turned his head toward Olivia, and gave the briefest of nods, the signal to start playing.

The music began—and then stopped.

Pretty Boy gasped.

"What's going on?" Maggie called out from below.

"The end pin of Eli's cello is sliding across the floor, taking the cello with it," said Pretty Boy. "Oh, no! I saw him practice last week. There were dozens of little holes in the wood floor, places for him to stick the end pin of his cello. But something happened to the floor. There's no place to stick the pin!"

Once again, Eli looked at Olivia and nodded. Once again they began and once again the cello went *whoosh,* like a skater slipping on the ice. The children didn't know what to do. Their teachers had prepared them for missed notes and for getting separated from each other. He hadn't anticipated a wayward cello.

"Where's Sam?" Maggie asked Pretty Boy. "Why isn't he doing something?"

Pretty Boy gazed back to where Sam had been sitting.

"Okay, Sam is standing up and trying to get past the people sitting next to him," he said. "At this rate it's going to take him too long to help Eli and Olivia out of this jam."

"Do something!" Maggie barked at Pretty Boy. Even though she couldn't see inside, the dog could hear that the respectful silence in the hall was turning uncomfortable.

If she'd been inside, she would have seen that Eli blushed when he heard some kids giggling. His worst nightmare was coming true!

So Pretty Boy did something. He slipped through the

window, hopped onto the stage, and trotted over to Eli. As if they'd planned it, the cat began to parade back and forth in front of the boy, grandly waving his tail like a giant fan.

At first Eli looked horrified, until he heard Olivia laughing. And she wasn't the only one.

"Look at that cat!" someone in the audience called out. "Is he part of the show?"

One woman whispered, "I thought no animals were allowed inside the school!"

"I don't know," said the man next to her. "But it's pretty funny, don't you think?"

Eli began to smile and pet Pretty Boy, who sat down next to him. By then, people were clapping their hands.

And Sam had made his way to the stage.

When Eli saw his teacher there, his smile began to droop. Was Sam going to yell at him in front of everyone?

Giving the boy a wink, Sam whispered, "Eli, I'm too old for this!" Then he knelt on the stage, grabbed hold of the end pin to steady it, and gave thumbs-up with the other.

Pretty Boy trotted back to the window, jumped onto

the sill, and scooted back outside to the tree branch.

Eli took a deep breath and nodded at Olivia. They began to play "Song of the Wind" as well as they ever had, with Sam crouched next to Eli, still as a statue.

Maggie hadn't been able to see what had happened, but she'd been listening closely. As the music wafted out the window, she growled in a low voice, "Nicely done."

Pretty Boy grinned and waved his tail as though he were still onstage.

"It was nothing," he said modestly.

CHAPTER EIGHTEEN

An Allergic Reaction

Pretty Boy was content. He couldn't imagine why he would ever need to change the way things were.

But Fate had a different plan.

It took one cough—and then another—to turn Pretty Boy's world upside down again.

Lilly had always been a sneezer. Her family was so used to it that sometimes they would say "bless you" when she entered a room—even if she hadn't sneezed.

But as summer approached the sneeze turned into a hacking cough that couldn't be ignored.

"We have to go to an allergist," her mother said to Lilly.

"I don't want to," said Lilly. "I'm fi . . ."

Before she could say "fine," she erupted into a coughing fit.

There was no more arguing. An appointment was made.

The allergist did all kinds of tests. When the results came, she called Lilly and her mother into her office.

"You are allergic to dust and certain flowers and trees and maybe a little bit to your dog," she began.

"So I'm fine, right doctor?" Lilly interrupted.

The doctor looked stern.

"No, not fine young lady," she said. "You have a serious allergy. To your cat."

Lilly burst into tears.

Her mother held Lilly in her arms. "Are you sure that's it?" she asked the doctor. "Pretty Boy has been living with us for a while now and Lilly started coughing recently."

The doctor nodded. "That isn't unusual," she said. "Sometimes it takes time for an allergy to gain strength."

Lilly squeezed her mother's hand.

"Is there anything we can do?" her mother asked the doctor.

"Well," said the doctor. "Easiest is to get rid of the cat . . ."

Lilly began to wail.

The doctor continued as though there weren't a desperate child crying in misery sitting right across from her.

". . . or," she said, "we can try to control Lilly's reaction."

"What do I have to do," asked Lilly? "I'll do anything?"

Her mother looked worried. "She won't have to take shots will she?"

The doctor sighed.

"Okay," she said. "We'll try it with no shots. You have to get rid of the cat's dander. That's the flaky skin that people react to with allergies."

For the next few weeks, twice a week, they immersed Pretty Boy in the tub—despite his objections to being soaked—and rubbed him vigorously with a brush. He was infuriated by this indignity. He yowled and squirmed. His tail grew huge, as though filling up with a flood of anger and frustration.

Lilly tried to explain. "Pretty Boy, we have to do this so you can stay with us," she said.

She broke into a coughing fit.

"You see," she said. "I'm allergic to you."

Pretty Boy's heart ached. "How could this be?" he thought. "How could someone you love be allergic to you? How can my beautiful fur be so harmful? What is wrong with me."

After that, he stood silently during the baths, though he couldn't stop his tail from expressing how he felt. The whole thing was humiliating!

In addition to the baths, Lilly's parents scrubbed Pretty Boy with a washcloth every night. They bought a special vacuum cleaner, which sucked up every stray white hair. Another machine purified the air.

Nothing worked. Lilly's cough didn't get better and may have even gotten worse.

"I want the shots," Lilly declared one day.

She was very brave, never flinching from the needle.

But she kept on coughing.

They tried a naturopath and an acupuncturist and then they tried a hypnotist.

But Lilly's allergies were stronger than all of them. Her cough continued to get worse.

The children's parents were torn. They, too, loved Pretty Boy, but they couldn't bear to listen to Lilly hack away all night long. She developed dark circles around her eyes from lack of sleep, and grew thinner and thinner from worry.

"I should leave," Pretty Boy said to Maggie one day. "I'm nothing but trouble."

Maggie placed a paw on Pretty Boy's back.

"You can't leave," she said. "Eli is depending on you. And Lilly loves you. If you go away, you'll break her heart."

Pretty Boy sniffed. "At least she'll be able to breathe!"

Maggie sighed. "There must be a way to figure this out."

Pretty Boy said glumly, "Yes, I should leave."

Maggie replied, "Something better than that."

Pretty Boy curled up into a ball. "Let me know when you have the answer."

The household grew tense. Pretty Boy had to stay as far away from Lilly as possible, not easy in an apartment. He missed listening to her nighttime stories. She cried herself to sleep, clutching the hypoallergenic stuffed cat her parents had bought for her. It was cute enough, but a poor substitute for the real thing.

Pretty Boy became distracted. One day, as Eli was practicing, the boy stopped playing and scolded the cat.

"What's wrong with you?" he asked. "You're completely off the beat."

Pretty Boy slumped to the floor and covered his head with his paws.

Eli put down his cello and knelt down to pet Pretty Boy.

"I'm sorry, boy," he said. "I know what's wrong. Stupid allergies. Things will be okay."

Pretty Boy wasn't so sure.

"What's going to happen to me?" he asked Maggie one day.

"Don't worry," she said. "Lilly loves you too much for them to send you away."

"What do you mean?" Pretty Boy asked. "Do you know something?"

"No," said Maggie. She wasn't lying, but she wasn't telling the entire truth. She had heard some discussions between the adults that caused her to worry. But she didn't want Pretty Boy to be upset because nothing was settled.

And then it happened. After dinner one evening, the children's parents called them into the living room.

"We've reached a decision," their father said. "We have to find another home for Pretty Boy."

"No!" yelled Eli. "Finally I kind of like New York and now you're ruining it."

He glared at Lilly, and then felt terrible when she broke into a coughing fit.

Pretty Boy looked at Maggie, who whimpered. Both animals sank to the floor without looking at the humans.

Like the children, Maggie and Pretty Boy didn't want to listen to the careful plan that had been worked out by their parents, night after sleepless night. They didn't want to hear the reassurances that Pretty Boy would be taken in only by someone approved by all of them. They didn't believe the promises that Pretty Boy would remain a part of their lives. The only thing that registered was the fact that Pretty Boy was here now and would be somewhere else in the very near future.

Their misery got worse as the parade of potential owners began.

First came the opera singer who lived in the building next door.

She seemed nice enough when she met Pretty Boy and Lilly liked the way she dressed.

"I understand you have perfect tempo," she said with a smile.

Pretty Boy was flattered.

She turned to Eli. "I've heard you play your cello," she said in a tone that implied she was talking very seriously, musician to musician. "Much improvement, much improvement."

Lilly whispered in Eli's ear. "This could be okay. She lives next door."

He nodded.

Then, without warning, the opera singer began to sing—"Memory" from *Cats*, the Broadway musical.

Pretty Boy couldn't explain why, but that song rubbed him the wrong way.

His back went up and he began to meow.

The singer thought he was encouraging her. She raised the volume and emotionality.

Pretty Boy couldn't help himself. He lifted his paw and scratched the singer on the leg.

She stopped singing and stared in horror at the tiny stream of blood running down her shin.

The children's parents apologized and scolded Pretty Boy, and then the room went silent.

The singer said quietly, "I guess Pretty Boy's review is in."

Then she stood up and said, "Sorry," as she headed toward the front door.

"Nice going," Maggie growled at Pretty Boy.

Pretty Boy didn't flinch.

"I couldn't bear to live with someone whose taste in music I can't stand," he said huffily.

Next came the man who answered the sign they'd posted at the music school. He had a shaggy mane of white hair and deep dark eyes.

He seemed promising, or maybe they thought that because he resembled Pretty Boy.

"I love cats," he began as he stroked Pretty Boy.

"My last cat, Esmeralda, was a genius, I feel sure of it," he said. "She was the most charming and beautiful creature you've ever seen."

They nodded politely.

"She woke me up every morning with the most musical meowing," he said. "She knew exactly what I needed, when to leave me alone and when to be there."

Pretty Boy looked worried.

The man continued. He described Esmeralda's talents, her sensitivities, her courage, and her grace.

His face grew very sad.

"There will never be another cat like her!" he said, and then burst into tears.

"Are you all right?" the children's mother asked.

He pulled out a large handkerchief and blew his nose.

"I'm fine," he said. "You'll have to excuse me."

Then he was gone.

Next came the know-it-all who proceeded to analyze Pretty Boy, then Maggie, and then the entire family, explaining in great detail what was wrong with each of them.

She was followed by a man who spoke so softly they couldn't hear a word he said.

The minute he left, Lilly couldn't help herself. She began to giggle. Eli joined in and soon they were all laughing out loud.

Pretty Boy realized it was the first time in weeks they'd been happy.

"Does this mean Pretty Boy can stay?" Lilly asked, looking so sweet her mother told herself never to forget that moment.

"No, sweetheart," she said, shaking her head. "It means we have to try harder to find the right person."

Pretty Boy listened and contemplated.

That night, after everyone was asleep, he leaped onto the windowsill and pushed open the screen, which was already loose.

Maggie stirred.

"What's going on," she mumbled, half awake and half asleep.

"I'm going, Maggie," Pretty Boy whispered. "Thank you for everything."

"Thank you, too," said Maggie, already back in dreamland. She would have no recollection of the conversation the next morning.

Pretty Boy made his way to Sixth Avenue, still filled with people though the hour was late. He was pausing to collect his thoughts when a bus stopped right in front of him. Pretty Boy stepped aside to avoid being trampled as a group poured out the exit. On impulse, the cat skittered onto the bus through the back door and slipped underneath a seat before anyone noticed him. The bus rumbled onward. Pretty Boy was on his own. Again.

CHAPTER NINETEEN
Matilda

Pretty Boy tried to drown out the noises of the bus with his inner music. But his old trick didn't work now. Instead of respite, the songs he conjured in his head only reminded him he wouldn't ever hear the Cello Man play again. And he couldn't stop himself from worrying: What about Eli? Pretty Boy didn't want to exaggerate his own importance, but he knew he helped the boy. And there was still so much to learn.

The cat groaned. He felt as if poor little Lilly's cough had blown apart his world, and now he had to start over again. How many times would he have to do this? He had heard the old saying about cats having nine lives, but who was doing the counting?

For quite a while no one came to the back of the bus where Pretty Boy lay huddled beneath a seat. Then a group of noisy tourists climbed aboard and filled several rows. All of a sudden a large map landed on the floor right next to Pretty Boy. The man who dropped it leaned over to pick it up, and shouted: *"Un chat, un chat!"*

Pretty Boy didn't understand French, but he quickly figured out the man was yelling at him. He scrambled into the aisle and under another seat, hoping the driver wouldn't notice.

Fat chance.

The tourists started laughing and pointing at *le chat*. Pretty Boy was so unnerved he began zigzagging from seat to seat, trying to get away.

It was hopeless. At the next stop, the driver got up from his seat, walked back through the bus, grabbed Pretty Boy, and tossed him out the front door.

"Sorry, fellow," he called out as he closed the bus doors. "No strays allowed."

Pretty Boy sat dejected on the curb.

"I'm not a stray," he thought. "I'm Pretty Boy."

To confirm, he stared down at the beautiful name tag Patti had given him.

But as he thought about his situation, he had to admit the bus driver had been accurate.

"I guess I am a stray," he mused.

He repeated the words: "I am a stray."

Stray.

How could such a short word make him feel so terrible?

"Stray is merely a word that describes my circumstance," he lectured himself.

He wasn't convinced.

Maybe it was unreasonable, but from the moment Patti gave him his name, he had been proud to be known as Pretty Boy. Or maybe he was just happy to be known.

Whatever the case, being called a stray made him feel dreadful, like he was nothing.

He felt sorry for himself. He was nothing and, so far as he knew, he was nowhere.

He sat meowing softly to himself, trying to avoid all the feet passing by. Finally he made his escape, running through the crowd on Sixth Avenue. At the next corner, he turned on to a block that was not so frenetic.

Pretty Boy didn't walk far along Forty-Fourth Street before he saw her.

All of a sudden, his mood lifted. Nowhere became less menacing.

The "her" in question was a large Ragdoll cat, with a beautiful brown and white face and startling blue eyes. Her fur, if possible, was even fluffier than Pretty Boy's.

She sat regally on the sidewalk, next to a man wearing a uniform.

It didn't take her long to notice that Pretty Boy was staring at her.

"Can I help you?" she asked in a voice that was accustomed to being obeyed, yet kind.

"You are lovely!" he blurted out.

She nodded. So many people had called her "lovely," "beautiful," and "gorgeous" that she thought of those words not as compliments but as descriptions.

Then she said, with a smile, "So are you."

He cocked his head.

"You look familiar," he said.

She lowered her eyes. "You might have seen me on television," she said. "I'm rather well known."

That's how Pretty Boy met Matilda, one of the most famous cats in New York. She descended from a long line of feline royalty, who had lived at the Algonquin Hotel since the 1930s.

"Want to come inside," she asked with a grin. Matilda was aware of her power.

Pretty Boy didn't want to seem too eager.

"Well, I have a few minutes," he said with a touch of his old swagger.

Matilda nodded at the man in the uniform, who was the hotel doorman. He gave a slight bow and opened the door wide enough for the two cats to pass through.

As they entered the hotel's grand lobby, Pretty Boy knew he wasn't downtown anymore. He had stepped into another century, when wealth was spelled out in plush and leather and dark wood.

He sat next to a potted palm near grand column and stared all around.

"Would you like a tour?" Matilda asked.

Their first stop was the Blue Bar, shadowy and glamorous, a place to reinvent yourself, at least for the duration of a drink. Pretty Boy already felt he had become someone else, though he couldn't say who, exactly.

He admired the drawings on the wall.

"What are these?" he asked.

"You don't know Al Hirschfeld's drawings?" Matilda asked, as if he'd admitted he didn't know the difference between the sun and the moon.

Pretty Boy was embarrassed but confessed that he didn't. He'd learned from Sam how important it was to admit you didn't know something.

Matilda told him all about the great cartoonist whose pen could capture a performer's essence in a few swift strokes. There was a period of time that actors and actresses measured how famous they were by whether they'd been the subject of a Hirschfeld caricature.

Pretty Boy saw that Matilda was not merely beautiful; she was an encyclopedia of literary lore. She was a magician, transforming mere furnishings into stage sets, a hotel dining room into romance itself.

Matilda told Pretty Boy about the hotel's famous Round Table, where a group of writers and critics met regularly during the 1920s to eat and amuse one another, usually when they were quite drunk.

"The hotel has capitalized very nicely on that legend," Matilda said with a conspiratorial meow. "People are so amusing. They think they'll become Dorothy Parker or F. Scott Fitzgerald if they meet here for dinner!"

Pretty Boy understood, even though he was not familiar with either of those writers. He peppered Matilda
with questions, because he was interested and because
he felt he could listen to her talk forever.

She seemed to like him, too.

Each moment they spent with each other was more
marvelous than the one before. Matilda told him
about her great-great-great-great-great-great-great-
great-grandfather—a stray, which had been taken in by
the hotel manager.

Pretty Boy interrupted.

"A stray?" he asked.

"Yes, but when he got cleaned up he was sleek and elegant," she said. "It's been a tradition in our family never to be too impressed by pedigree."

Matilda continued.

"A famous actor of the day named him Hamlet," she giggled. "That's how I've always known the only thing that may separate a stray from a prince is a good brushing."

She was the most extraordinary creature! Pretty Boy felt encouraged to tell Matilda about his adventures, how he had been homeless and was rescued. He told her about Patti and Dee and Roxie and the unexpected trip to Maine. And yes, he told her about the moose.

She was mesmerized by the danger he had faced.

"I've lived such a pampered life compared with you," she said with admiration. "You are very brave."

Pretty Boy was flattered and surprised. He'd thought of himself as artistic, intelligent, and good-looking— but never brave.

She wanted to know everything. He told her about the friends who had helped him, about the Cello Man and how he, Pretty Boy, had been helping Eli with his lessons.

"You've been doing important work," Matilda said gravely. "A great teacher is the link between the past and the future."

Pretty Boy felt compelled to correct her. "Sam is the teacher," he said. "I am the assistant."

"Oh, Pretty Boy," sighed Matilda. "You are quite a cat."

For the next few days they were inseparable. Sometimes they would meet other cats who were traveling with hotel guests. But Matilda warned Pretty Boy he should keep out of sight of the concierge. He was a nice enough fellow but a stickler for rules. Pretty Boy wasn't the first friend Matilda had brought home. The concierge had reminded her before that the Algonquin tradition only allowed for one hotel cat, not two.

Pretty Boy didn't mind lying low. He preferred to be alone with Matilda. They had so much to talk about.

As Matilda grew to know Pretty Boy better, she saw that he was both happy and unhappy. He missed his life downtown.

One morning, while Pretty Boy was still asleep, Matilda came to a decision.

When he woke up, she told him she had a special plan for their evening prowl.

Speaking with mock grandeur, she said. "I'm going to show you my favorite New York landmark."

When night fell, they walked over to Fifth Avenue and a couple of blocks south.

In front of them stood a massive building, vast and white, with magnificent arches and giant pillars.

"That's the New York Public Library," declared Matilda, with pride and reverence, as though she were introducing a queen.

Pretty Boy's eyes misted over.

"What's wrong?" Matilda asked.

"Nothing at all," he said. "It reminds me of the Washington Square Arch."

Matilda shook her head. "I don't know about that," she said. "But let's go closer."

When the traffic light turned, they scampered across the street.

"Look on top of those pedestals," Matilda ordered.

Pretty Boy obeyed, craning his neck for the best view possible. His effort was rewarded. He felt overwhelmed as his eyes took in the sight of two heroic marble lions.

"Their names are Patience and Fortitude," said Matilda. "They are the library's guardians."

Pretty Boy felt grander by association. It was as though he had grown taller and stronger and smarter just being in their presence. Being a cat had never felt more noble.

"Come on," Matilda urged him. "There's something else I have to show you."

They walked a block farther and turned onto 41st Street.

They hadn't gone far when Matilda asked, "Notice anything?"

Pretty Boy looked side to side and up and down.

He shook his head.

Matilda laughed.

"Look down!" she said.

Every few feet, there was a brass plaque with words on it, embedded into the sidewalk.

"What's this?" Pretty Boy asked.

"It's the Library Walk," Matilda explained. "Each one of these plaques has a famous quote from literature and poetry."

Pretty Boy was thrilled. "Thank you, Matilda," he said.

"Wait," she said. "There's a special plaque I want you to see."

She counted until they got to the seventh one.

"A well-known writer brought me here once when he was a guest of the hotel," she said. "I memorized the words."

She recited them.

"Everything is only for a day, both that which remembers and that which is remembered," she said.

"Who wrote that," Pretty Boy asked.

"A Roman emperor and philosopher named Marcus Aurelius Antoninus," Matilda replied. As a hotel cat, she had acquired the raconteur's ability to turn a few tidbits of information into the appearance of a vast store of knowledge.

"What do you think it means?" Pretty Boy asked.

Matilda looked at him tenderly.

"Let's go back to the Algonquin and I'll tell you," she said.

As she trotted off, he followed. In their short time together, he had learned that Matilda had inherited her ancestor Hamlet's theatrical bent. She believed in the importance of setting the stage, and Pretty Boy believed in Matilda.

CHAPTER TWENTY

Fermata

While Matilda was introducing Pretty Boy to a different side of the city, downtown things were gloomy.

"You look like a sack of potatoes," Sam greeted Eli when the boy arrived for his cello lesson a few days after Pretty Boy disappeared.

This observation wasn't polite, but it was accurate. The boy seemed to sag from top to bottom.

Eli shrugged his shoulders and bit his lips together. He hadn't been able to tell anyone what had happened—not even Olivia.

Sam glanced out the window.

"Where's your cat?" he asked.

Eli shrugged again.

The teacher decided the best thing to do was begin the lesson.

Eli began to play an étude, and then reached a symbol he didn't understand. It looked like a bird's eye.

"What is that?" he asked Sam.

The old man replied, "That's a fermata. It gives players the choice of holding a note as long as they want. Most people use it to make the note last longer, like something they don't want to give up."

He looked at Eli and said, "At my age, I want to put a fermata on everything."

"So do I!" Eli said with a catch in his voice.

Sam shook his head.

"No you don't my boy," he said. "You might feel like it sometime, but that would make a pretty dull piece of music"

"I'm not talking about music," Eli said. "I'm talking about Pretty Boy."

Sam waited.

Eli began to talk and talk, words coming out like water from a broken faucet. He told Sam everything—

about Lilly's allergies and the awful people who came to audition to be Pretty Boy's family and how they drove Pretty Boy away.

"He understood what was going on!" the boy exclaimed. "He knew we were abandoning him! He must have. Why else would he leave?"

Sam stared out the window and noticed how blue the sky was. No matter how old he got, he was always surprised when the weather didn't conform to the way he felt. Why wasn't it gray and overcast?

"You could be right, Eli," he said. "That's a very smart cat. Smart enough to take care of himself."

They sat in silence for a few minutes and then Eli began to play. When he reached the fermata, he held the note a very long time.

When Pretty Boy and Matilda returned to the Algonquin from their walk, they found a delicious bowl of cream waiting for them outside the kitchen.

The two cats lapped up the treat in companionable silence. Then they nestled against each other in Matilda's basket and took a nap.

When Pretty Boy woke up he felt someone's eyes

on him. It was Matilda, looking at him with a strange expression, part affection and part something Pretty Boy couldn't identify.

"What is it?" he meowed, and affectionately batted her head with his paw.

"Pretty Boy," Matilda said, "I'll never forget what a wonderful time we've had together."

Pretty Boy was alarmed.

"What do you mean you'll never forget?" Pretty Boy asked. "Why *should* you forget? I'm still here."

It didn't take him long to answer his own question.

"Why do you want me to go?" he asked. "Why?"

"I could make up some wise saying for you to repeat to yourself when the moon rises over Washington Square," said Matilda. "I could tell you I don't want to spoil the wonderful time we've had together by making it last too long. But that would be a lie. I would be happy to have you with me forever, but then I would have to leave the Algonquin. Remember, there's only room for one cat at the hotel."

"So leave!" Pretty Boy cried out.

Matilda shook her head.

"I can't," she said. "I belong here. And I know something else. You belong downtown, with all the people who depend on you. You have a job to do."

Pretty Boy wanted to retort, That's ridiculous! I'm a cat.

But he didn't reply because he realized Matilda understood something important about him that he didn't want to admit. He did miss the children and the dogs and the Cello Man. He missed Washington Square and the dog run. He even missed the hawk!

It seemed terribly unfair. He finally met someone who knew his thoughts better than he did, and she was telling him they had to go their separate ways.

"Everything is only for a day," she reminded him. "But these days will last forever because I'll never forget them."

"That stinks," he said.

Then he added a practical objection.

"I don't even know how to get back downtown," he said.

"I do," Matilda said. "Come with me."

He followed her to the hotel lobby and to the concierge's desk, where Matilda began to make a loud racket. She yowled and screeched. Pretty Boy was astounded that such horrible sounds could come out of such a beautiful creature. His admiration for Matilda grew even bigger, even though her ferocity was frightening.

The concierge leaned across his desk and looked down at her.

"What's going on, Matilda?" he asked.

She walked over to Pretty Boy and whacked him across the head with her paw.

Pretty Boy was stunned—until he saw Matilda give him a wink.

"Who's that?" the concierge said. "I'll grab that stray."

Before Pretty Boy knew what was happening, the concierge had grabbed him by the scruff of his neck and was heading toward the door. Pretty Boy's legs swirled through the air like eggbeaters. The doorman tipped his hat at the concierge. As he opened the door, a little girl entering the hotel called out.

"Look at that beautiful cat," she said. "I love his velvet collar. Can I pet him?"

The concierge grunted.

"Can she?" the girl's mother asked.

"All right," said the concierge grumpily.

As the little girl stroked Pretty Boy's fur, she said to her mother, "Look at this pretty tag."

"Tag?" said the concierge.

"Look!" said the little girl.

The concierge looked and saw a name and number engraved there. A few minutes later, Eli and Lilly's mother picked up her phone.

"What?" she said, a smile breaking through the mournful look that had been stuck on her face since Pretty Boy left.

"He's where?!"

She began to laugh.

"Yes, we'll come get him," she said.

As this conversation was taking place, Pretty Boy angrily asked Matilda, "What made you so sure the concierge would see my tag? I could have ended up at the pound. I thought you cared about me!"

Matilda's calm answer made Pretty Boy love her even more.

"Pretty Boy," she said in her clear voice. "I care about you a great deal and would never do anything to harm you. Trust me, I knew this would work out for the best."

Matilda had been correct about everything. Pretty Boy never forgot their time together. Sometimes she appeared in his mind with so much clarity he blinked, uncertain whether he was seeing her or remembering her. Most of the time, these appearances added a sweet overtone to his comings and goings, the way the cherry blossoms in Washington Square reminded him of Patti and Roxie. But sometimes thinking of Matilda made him feel angry and confused. Why did they have to follow their separate paths, as Matilda insisted?

Pretty Boy never was able to answer this question to his satisfaction. But he felt his life was full.

His homecoming had been joyful. Pretty Boy was hugged and praised and brushed into satisfied exhaustion. Lilly coughed and sneezed, but everyone pretended not to notice. The children's parents knew they would have to find someone to take care of Pretty Boy but decided to delay as long as they could.

Then Pretty Boy solved the problem himself, quite unexpectedly.

At Eli's next cello lesson, Sam was delighted to see Pretty Boy had returned.

"I'm still worried," said Eli. "My sister's cough is getting worse. We'll have to do something."

Sam looked surprised at the words that came out of his own mouth.

"Pretty Boy could live with me," he said.

Eli was shocked. For reasons he couldn't explain, his cello teacher didn't seem like the kind of person who would own a pet. At that moment, Eli grew up a little as he realized that his teacher had a large and unknown life outside the music room.

"I used to have a dog," Sam said, "and then a cat.

But after my children grew up and my wife died, I didn't want the responsibility."

The old man looked at Pretty Boy, sitting on the floor between them, and smiled.

"After you told me that Pretty Boy had run away, I felt down in the dumps all day," Sam said. "At first I thought it was indigestion or the weather. Then I realized I was lonely. Usually I don't let myself think that way. But the thought of never seeing your friend again . . ."

He stopped. Eli noticed that Sam's face was like a statue's, holding history and secrets that the boy suddenly wanted to know. But he also seemed outside of time, forever young, ready for adventure.

"I'd be glad to be Pretty Boy's custodian," Sam said.

"Custodian?" Eli asked.

"I mean I'll take care of him but he will still belong to you and your sister," Sam said. "As much as anyone can belong to anyone."

Pretty Boy had been listening intently. He liked the way the conversation was going.

"Could he still go to the dog park with Maggie?" Eli asked.

Sam laughed. "I don't know why not," he said.

It didn't take long for the cat and the musician to

fall into a comfortable routine, as Pretty Boy came to grasp the pattern of Sam's days. Every morning, without fail, the old man sat up in bed and rubbed his fingers, muttering that his hands ached from arthritis. Then he slowly showered, shaved, and dressed in his somewhat formal style. After a small healthy breakfast of toast, berries, yogurt, and coffee with milk, Sam took a walk around the neighborhood. Pretty Boy usually went along, always noticing the positive effect of this morning constitutional on Sam's spirits as well as his posture. His head became more erect and his pace quickened.

When they returned, Sam sat on a chair by a window and played his cello.

He never skipped this routine. Pretty Boy understood that music had become his pulse, the way he measured his heart rate, the way he knew he was alive.

Pretty Boy's happiest days were spent in Washington Square, where he became a fixture, keeping time to the Cello Man's music with his tail.

His proudest moment came the day Eli stopped by carrying his cello. By then the boy was old enough to come to the park himself, and tall enough to play a full-size cello.

"Can I join you?" he asked the Cello Man.

"What's taken you so long?" Sam replied. "I've been waiting for you."

Pretty Boy cued them with his tail, and they began to play. The music floated above the city's honks and shrieks, all the way to the top of Bobst Library, where a red-tailed hawk stared down—and then turned to drop a piece of food into his chick's tiny beak.

In retrospect, it all made sense, as though Pretty Boy had been planning things to turn out this way all along.

ACKNOWLEDGMENTS

First, thanks to Debra Woodward for telling us about a real cat named Pretty Boy, who inspired our story. Our deepest appreciation goes to our families for their love and support; our editors Nancy Conescu and Lily Malcom for their most helpful suggestions; Rosanne Lauer for her careful copyedit; Jasmin Rubero for being available for every production question; Barry Kramer for his sharp eye; Lauri Hornik for publishing us so happily; and the indefatigable Kathy Robbins, who is always there for us. Gratitude beyond measure to Jeffrey Ziegler, Peter Lewy, Irene Sharp, and Samuel Reiner, whose love of music and passion for cello has tipped the world's balance toward beauty.